PRAISE FOR THE SHERRI TRAVI[S]

"A series that gives the reader a casual style and storytelling with staying power. The pacing is that of a southern drawl, with a core of beer, bars and bad behavior."

—*The Hamilton Spectator*

"The Sherri Travis Mysteries started out well and have gotten better . . . the writing keeps getting tighter, and Smallman knows how to crank up the reader's tension. One can't help wanting more and anticipating the next book in this entertaining and fast-paced series." —*National Post*

"Smallman, winner of the Unhanged Arthur Ellis for her first Travis novel, is at the top of her game." —*The Globe and Mail*

"Phyllis Smallman is a gifted writer, and has a strong and captivating protagonist in Sherri Travis. Sherri is an engaging figure whose combination of single-minded determination, absolute candor and underlying sense of values utterly beguiles the reader. A fascinating read." —*The Sherbrooke Record*

"A murder-mystery crossed with chick-lit, this book is a lot of fun."

—Her Free Reads Blog

"High tension, wonderful descriptions of the Florida countryside and a very real, heartbreaking theme of man's inhumanity toward man . . . a must read."

—Mystery & Me Blog

"Wonderful mysteries." —Harriet Klausner, Amazon.com

"Snappy dialog, rapid pacing and characters you'd love to meet in a beach bar."

—*Winnipeg Free Press*

HIGHBALL EXIT

ALSO BY PHYLLIS SMALLMAN

Sherri Travis Mysteries
Margarita Nights
Sex in a Sidecar
A Brewski for the Old Man
Champagne for Buzzards

HIGHBALL EXIT

PHYLLIS SMALLMAN

TouchWood
Editions

TouchWood Editions
touchwoodeditions.com

LIBRARY AND ARCHIVES CANADA CATALOGUING IN PUBLICATION
Smallman, Phyllis
Highball exit / Phyllis Smallman.

(A Sherri Travis mystery)
ISBN 978-1-927129-79-1

I. Title. II. Series: Smallman, Phyllis. Sherri Travis mystery.

PS8637.M36H54 2012   C813'.6   C2012-904826-7

Proofreader: Lenore Hietkamp
Cover and interior design: Tania Craan
Author photo: Linda Matteson-Reynolds

BRITISH COLUMBIA ARTS COUNCIL   Canada Council for the Arts   Conseil des Arts du Canada   Canadian Heritage   Patrimoine canadien

We gratefully acknowledge the financial support for our publishing activities from the Government of Canada through the Canada Book Fund, Canada Council for the Arts, and the province of British Columbia through the British Columbia Arts Council and the Book Publishing Tax Credit.

MIX
Paper from responsible sources
FSC® C016245

The interior pages of this book have been printed on 100% post-consumer recycled paper, processed chlorine free, and printed with vegetable-based inks.

This book is a work of fiction. Names, characters, places, and incidents are either products of the author's imagination or are used fictitiously. Any resemblance to actual events or locales or persons, living or dead, is entirely coincidental.

1 2 3 4 5 16 15 14 13 12

PRINTED IN CANADA

For Elle Wild
~ with much love and gratitude ~

CHAPTER 1

It was Sunday morning and I was out on the lanai of my borrowed beach house, sprawled in a canvas lawn chair, the Sunday *Herald* discarded at my feet. The bright Florida sun was giving me a headache. I couldn't find the energy to go inside the air-conditioned house or even move into its shade. I'd surrendered to lethargy and given up on everything but breathing.

The September air was heavy with humidity. At ten o'clock in the morning, the temperature already hovered around ninety, with a forecast for worse to come. Overhead small white clouds, eager to be gone, rushed across the sky, leaving nothing behind but the drought that wouldn't end.

Elvis flew in with wings extended, neck out and long legs dangling, and came to a running stop. He stepped delicately onto the listing concrete squares and stood there with his head twitching right, then left, and then back again.

"What, do you want . . . applause?"

He cranked his neck around and gave me the evil eye.

"I'm no tourist. I knew you could do it."

Elvis tilted his head to the side.

"Go away you moocher. I'm the only one getting a handout today."

He lifted a stick leg and paused before he set it gingerly down and inched closer.

"There isn't a scrap in that fridge."

He cocked his head, one yellow eye considering me as his fine white feathers quivered in the light breeze.

"If there was a hotdog in there I'd eat it myself." Elvis was the only egret in all Florida who preferred hotdogs to fish. He couldn't abide those disgusting things no matter how hungry he was.

"Get lost, freak."

Elvis decided I was suffering from a serious lack of charity and lifted off with a squawk of protest to fly north across the sand dunes, back towards Jacaranda, looking for someone more generous than me.

This tiny aqua bungalow, on the beach in Jacaranda, was built closer to the edge of the Gulf of Mexico than the new laws allowed. Sand dunes and beach grasses were the only things I could see from the patio. It didn't matter, all the other beach houses were empty until the season started. I was alone in paradise, solitary and miserable.

Even the chartreuse gecko darting in and out of the clay pots full of dead flowers couldn't lift my mood. My business . . . no, my life, the Sunset Bar and Grill, was running on borrowed money and the fumes of my dying dreams.

I kept telling myself that everything would go back to normal when the long line of cars with out of state license plates started arriving. The winter before, the tourist trade had been down, leaving me pirouetting on the edge of bankruptcy, and now I'd reached a crisis point. The Sunset needed an infusion of cash or it wouldn't survive.

If I could just last until after Thanksgiving, two more months, I stood a chance of keeping the bank from stepping in. But this nasty, nasty little voice in my head kept saying, "And what if the tourists don't come? What if this is the new normal . . . the new state of things?" God, I hate that little voice. It keeps insisting on pointing out truths I'm quite capable of avoiding.

I tried to think of someone to tap for money, considered all my options, and discovered there weren't any. When you grow up in a trailer park on the edge of a swamp, you just don't make the right social connections to stave off insolvency.

It was time to make a new plan and decide what I was going to do when it all went down the tubes. I'd read every line in the Help Wanted section of the *Herald*, but nobody wanted bartenders, my only marketable skill.

So there I sat identifying the expendable—which server I'd let go and what supplier I could string out a little longer—when I heard a car pull in on the crushed-shell driveway. Glad to be distracted from my wretchedness, I went inside to see who my visitor was.

A police car was parked outside the kitchen window.

CHAPTER 2

The back door of the cruiser opened. A swollen ankle in a white sneaker appeared below the door. A few seconds later the second foot followed. It took a little more time for the stout figure to pull herself to her feet.

I gripped the edge of the sink and stared at her as my world went tilt. Everything outside looked so bright and ordinary, but I knew the truth. Elderly ladies don't come visiting in police cars.

Aunt Kay was overweight, maybe even obese. Two black raisin eyes peered out of her rice pudding face while her salt and pepper hair sprang up from her head in an uncontrolled tangle of steel wool. Holding onto the top of the door with both hands, she stepped around it, slamming it behind her without ever taking her eyes off the kitchen window.

She was dressed in cropped beige pants and a square-cut orange flowered blouse, an outfit that did nothing to enhance her appearance. But looks had never been the important thing about Aunt Kay. She had something far rarer than beauty; she was easy to love.

Frozen in front of the window, I watched her uneven gait as she made her way to the house. My brain was doing a quick survey of potential disasters and came up with too many possibilities to make speculation worthwhile.

When she reached the carport and disappeared from my sight, I rushed to the kitchen door. I stepped out onto the small stoop, holding the screen door open with my butt, and waited as she pulled herself up the rickety wooden steps on knees that no longer bent.

Aunt Kay stopped at the top, gave me a weak smile, and turned to wave at the police car. The cop saluted and reversed out onto Beach Road.

"What are you doing here?" I reached out and kissed her smooth cheek and hugged her, smelling the familiar odor of rose-scented talc. The fragrance brought back feelings of comfort and safety. Aunt Kay had been my afterschool caregiver through most of grade school, and my weekend minder while my mother worked and Tully Jenkins, my mostly absent father, was either in disgrace or hauling oranges north.

I liked going to Aunt Kay's house. It was close to my best friend Marley Hemming's house and there was always a jumble of kids to play with. Later, when I was too old to need watching and an abusive man moved in with my mother, Aunt Kay's was my safe place to hide from his hands. She never turned me away or pushed me to tell her what was bothering me. She just accepted that I needed to be there.

"What's happened?" I was desperate to hear the worst now, needed to know the full extent of the nameless horror about to crash into me. "Why is a cop delivering you to my door? Why are you here?"

I tried to hug her again but Aunt Kay shook me off. "Oh for goodness' sake, Sherri, give me a minute."

I held the door while she went inside, dropped her bag on the table, took a deep breath, and then let the air out all in a rush. "I wanted to tell you before you heard it from someone else."

I waited, my mind chasing shadows. Someone had to be dead. My first thought was Clay. But he was up north at Cedar Key and Aunt Kay barely knew him.

It couldn't be Marley. She was out at the ranch with Tully and if either of them were dead the other would have called. But what if they were both dead?

I reached out to touch Aunt Kay's arm. It felt chilled and damp, like her blood had gone cold. "Just tell me."

"It's Holly."

"Holly Mitchell?" I said the name just to be sure I had the right person . . . that I'd heard correctly.

Aunt Kay nodded. "She's dead."

"She can't be! Holly's too young." Silly thing to say—being twenty-one is no protection from death. "Was it an accident?"

Aunt Kay looked away and her lip quivered.

CHAPTER 3

"The police came," she said. "They found my telephone number in her wallet. She listed me as next of kin on one of those little ID things that come with wallets."

She leaned forward, the edge of the table cutting into her breasts. "Isn't that the saddest thing you ever heard? To think I was the closest thing to a relative she had."

"How?" I asked. "How did she die?"

She pulled back from the table and her eyes dropped. Her left thumb found a hangnail and began worrying it.

"Tell me."

"It seems she committed suicide, took a highball of drugs." Tears slid down her cheeks.

I got a box of tissues off the top of the fridge and set it on the table between us.

I wanted to ask if there could be a mistake. "She was so unendingly cheerful. How could someone with that optimistic outlook kill themselves?"

"The policeman who came to tell me about Holly's death took me to Sarasota to make the official identification." She sucked in her lips and bit down, struggling for control.

"They showed me her note, on pink paper. She always loved pink."

"I remember." When I first took over the Sunset, and was still feeling my way into the job, Aunt Kay called and insisted I hire Holly.

Aunt Kay had no pride when it came to begging jobs for the people who grew up in her backyard. We all knew if we needed it she'd do the same for us, her love making us part of a small and unique tribe.

"They took me to the morgue. I didn't know it was her at first. Holly's hair was stark black. You know how she was, a new color every week. I hadn't seen this one. I haven't seen her in months. She looked so small and fragile, like some discarded porcelain doll . . . so thin. Her face . . ." Her hand rose to her own cheeks. "Holly's face was all bruised. Someone had beaten her."

"Oh shit."

"There's something else worrying me." Aunt Kay's eyes were locked on mine. "No one knows what happened to her baby."

CHAPTER 4

"Baby? Holly didn't have a baby." Why was I so sure of this? Maybe because spiked magenta hair and a glittering nose stud were not included in my vision of motherhood.

"Oh, there was a baby all right," Aunt Kay said, nodding her head.

How long had I known Aunt Kay? Almost all of my thirty-one years—was her mind starting to wobble? Perhaps the shock of Holly's death had been too much for her.

"I'm not losing my mind." Her piercing black eyes held mine. "Angel was born about Christmas and Holly borrowed a car and brought her to Jacaranda in January or early February. Holly wanted me to take care of Angel full-time . . . until she worked some things out."

"She had no right to ask that of you."

"Holly said it would only be for a few months." Her mouth worked in and out and her hands worried each other. "I said no. Today I asked the police about the baby. They said there wasn't any baby, said there was no sign of a baby in the apartment."

"Perhaps Holly found someone else to care for the child, maybe her parents."

Aunt Kay shook her head. "A few months ago Marnie Mitchell moved back to Jacaranda and started working behind the beauty counter at my local Walgreen store. I asked her about Holly's little girl and

9

she stared at me like I'd lost my mind. She said Holly didn't have any children. Got all sweet and started doing the 'There, there' thing we do with people suffering from dementia, and told me I was confused."

"Maybe Holly gave her baby up for adoption."

She gave a grimace of annoyance and leaned towards me, trying to make me understand. "Holly only wanted me to take Angel for a couple of months. She said that everything was going to change soon . . . that all her dreams were coming true. She was real excited, so sure things were finally working out for her. She thought her big break had arrived."

"Sounds like horse feathers to me."

"Yes, I thought so too. Holly, well, she . . ." Aunt Kay was searching for nice words to say that Holly had nothing but stale air between her ears and operated from hope rather than common sense. "Holly was never practical. She needed me and I let her down."

"You had a perfect right to say no if you didn't want to care for another child."

"It wasn't that. It wasn't that I didn't want to help her. I couldn't."

"Couldn't?"

She sighed. "Life can play strange tricks."

"And what particular prank did it pull on you, Aunt Kay?"

"Just age and a body that won't co-operate anymore. Time seems to be having its way with me. I always knew life was a terminal condition, but . . ." She wrinkled her nose and shrugged without finishing her thought. "I've been having some problems. It's my heart you see; seems I was born with something called Wolff-Parkinson-White syndrome. The thing is, my heart is just worn out. I can't be responsible for children anymore, can't even drive a car."

"I'm so sorry."

She reached across the table and took my hand. "I know." She patted my hand. "I don't mind so much, it's just this waiting, no family, no one needing me." She sat back in her chair. "I loved Holly like my own child. I need to know what happened to her and I want you to help me find out."

"Aunt Kay, I'm trying to keep my restaurant alive and filling in for staff I can't afford to replace. I haven't got time to help you. I'm so sorry."

She nodded and looked around the kitchen. "So, house on the beach—I suppose that means you have lots of money?"

My laugh was a bitter sound. "You know better. This place is on loan until December when the real owners show up."

"And that rich man you've been dating . . . Is he going to help you save the Sunset?"

I kept my mouth shut. Clay had lost nearly everything in the housing collapse. The penthouse was gone, as was his real estate company, and all he had left was his failing development in Cedar Key and the ranch, which wasn't worth what he paid for it.

"Everything's going good for Sherri Travis, is it?"

There was no turning away from her piercing gaze and no lying. "This isn't the best time for us. I'm behind on the mortgage on the Sunset and I'm working from when the Sunset opens until we close. I already told you I can't help you."

Her face grew sunny. "Now perhaps we can help each other." Planting her hands on the table, Aunt Kay pushed herself to her feet. "Where's the bathroom, dear?"

She'd baited her hook and now she was going to let me swim around looking at the lure, getting hungry and ready to bite at anything. But I knew her well enough to look for the barb in the delicacy she dangled in front of me before I nibbled.

I pointed. "Down the hall, second door on the right."

She walked slowly and carefully away from me. Time had been unkind to Aunt Kay. The edges of her shoes cut cruelly into her flesh and her movements were old and cautious. When had she aged? I suppose it was when I stopped watching. Did she notice the same changes in me?

My cell phone rang and I warily checked the number. My chicken supplier, as desperate as I was, had taken to calling at odd times of the day and night in his pursuit of payment.

The call display said it was from Isaak, the Sunset's chef.

"Why are you calling? You're on holiday. What's wrong?"

"No 'hello'? No 'I missed you'?"

"Somehow, Isaak, I don't think you called to say you're missing me and I don't think you've spent your time in Washington thinking about the Sunset."

He sighed. "*Chérie*, I've been offered a job here."

There it was, the final black line under "the end" for me and my dreams. Looking out the window, the sea grapes grew bleary.

I was still standing at the window, staring out with unseeing eyes, when Aunt Kay said, "Sherri."

I jumped.

"Sorry, sorry." She reached out a hand. "Are you all right? You look . . . well, sort of funny." She canted her head to the right and considered me. "Things really aren't going well for you, are they?"

I crossed my arms and leaned back against the counter. "What were you saying about us helping each other?"

She turned away and went to the table and eased her backside down on a chair. "It's Angel."

She smiled up at me and gave a little nod of confirmation, knowing she'd hooked me. "I want to know Holly's baby is safe."

"Maybe the baby was another of Holly's fantasies." The betrayal and resentment I felt after Isaak's phone call was now directed at

Holly. "She was always making up stories about famous people she'd met, always exaggerating the truth."

Aunt Kay shook her head. "That baby was no fantasy. I saw her . . . lovely red curls."

"Maybe it was someone else's baby."

She glared up at me. "You think she could fool me?"

"Nope, none of us ever could." I pushed away from the counter. "Who's the father then?"

"That's the second problem."

The worry in her voice galvanized my attention. "Problem? How?"

"At the morgue, I asked who found Holly."

We stared into each other's eyes and I waited for the next piece of bad news.

"I was told that it was a policeman, an Officer Raines."

I sighed with regret and slumped down at the table to listen.

CHAPTER 5

Dan Raines lived next door to Aunt Kay and found his playmates among the clutter of toys and kids in her yard.

"Holly lived two doors down from Dan," Aunt Kay said. "She worshiped him and told everyone she was going to marry him someday."

"If he found the body, why wouldn't he identify Holly?"

"Exactly."

"Did you tell the other policeman, the one who picked you up, about Dan?"

She looked uncomfortable. "I thought it would be best not to until I knew why Dan hadn't told them. He must have had a reason not to admit he knew Holly."

"Maybe it was another Officer Raines; maybe there are two cops with the same name."

She gave me the dimwitted-child look I often got from my teachers.

"How likely is that? In any case, if it was a different police officer, Dan will have to be told about Holly."

Dim but not stupid—I knew when I was being set up. "You can just call and talk to him. You don't need me for that."

"This isn't something you can do over the phone," she protested. "I want you to go up to Sarasota and talk to him face to face." She

14

frowned. "I'd go with you but you'll do better on your own. He'll be more honest with you."

"Look, Aunt Kay, I know you're upset about this, even feel some kind of responsibility, but you shouldn't. Let the police sort it out."

"Won't you amuse an old woman, an old friend?" She looked at me with such great sincerity that I almost expected her to put her hand on her heart. I already assumed her talk of being ill was a lie to get me to go along with what she wanted.

She spread her hands wide, palms up. "I was looking at Holly, lying there all bruised and battered, and I could only think of one thing: where's her baby?" She leaned towards me. "There are so many questions I need answers to. Does Holly being beaten have anything to do with Angel being gone? Who's looking after Angel and is she waiting for her mother to come for her?"

"Speak to the police."

"I did. The police didn't pay any attention to me. I told them about the baby, tried to get them interested, but they aren't going any further because Holly left a suicide note. It's closed. They're going to do an autopsy but they're sure she took her own life. That ends it for them."

"So what do you want from me exactly?"

"I want you to help me find Angel."

"You might just as well ask me to find a cure for cancer. I wouldn't know where to start."

"But you're smart and you understand people. They trust you, always have. They open up to you and they tell you things. I can't drive anymore, because of my condition, but I'll go with you." Her face lit up at the prospect. "People ignore old ladies. And they don't care if we ask stupid questions. We'll find Angel."

"I have to warn you, I haven't a lot of time for this."

She picked up a spoon, turning it over between her fingers. "Oh, yes . . . time . . . well, I haven't got a lot of it myself."

"And what makes you think I'll give in to blackmail?"

She smiled. "Because you were always compassionate and because I'll pay you . . ." she stopped and considered the amount, watching me and assessing what would tempt me, ". . . three months' mortgage for one week of your time."

She had my attention now. "Really?"

"Really. I go in next week for a little procedure, so you see both of us are running out of time."

Maybe it was even true or maybe she just wanted to convince me, but either way she needn't have bothered. She had me with three months' mortgage.

CHAPTER 6

"One week of my time for three months of mortgage?"

"Exactly."

"That's crazy."

"Remember when I was saying I didn't know what to do with myself? Well, this is what I want to do. I don't want to go on a cruise, don't even want to go to a resort, but you wouldn't think it was wrong for me to spend money on that kind of thing, would you? I want to find Angel and I want to know what happened to Holly to make her take her own life."

"Why don't you hire a private investigator?"

"And sit at home waiting for news? I want to be there."

I started to speak but she held up a hand to stop me.

"I have another reason. My sister committed suicide. It's a terrible thing." Her voice was soft. "For those who are left behind it's never-ending pain." She looked down at the table and watched her forefinger go round and round in tiny circles while she took deep breaths. "The anger and the guilt never go away and you never understand. Please, Sherri, help me."

"You're paying me a lot of money."

"Money isn't my main concern at the moment but . . ." She raised a finger to stop me from speaking. "I want to make sure you're committed to this. If you think you can go into this half-hearted, making calming noises while you go on worrying about your restaurant, think again. I'm going to give you a postdated check and if I think you aren't paying attention, not putting your brain into this, I'll cancel it."

I bit back angry words and took a deep breath. "It hurts me that you don't trust me."

For the first time she laughed. "I've known you since you were five. You're never more sincere than when you're lying or when you have no intention of doing what you've been told to do. I've watched you say, 'Yes, Auntie,' and then go right on doing what you wanted to, the very thing I just told you not to do."

She leaned towards me and pointed her finger at me. "I want you paying attention and concentrating on this."

"What exactly do you want me to do?"

She started counting off the steps on her fingers. "First, go see Dan and find out if he was the one who found Holly and if so, why did he find her? Seems like a big coincidence if he was the one who discovered her. See if he knows anything about what happened to Holly over these last few months. If he doesn't know, maybe he can find out."

"Clay is coming home today, the first time he's been back in two weeks. Can it wait until tomorrow? I'm all yours then."

Her lips pursed. "See, that's what I mean." For a moment I thought I'd already blown it. At last she gave me a little nod. "Tomorrow I think we should go see the apartment where Holly died. It's up in Sarasota. The nice policeman gave me her address. It's in a section of town where the streets are all named after tropical fruit." She opened her handbag and pulled out a slip of paper and read off the address.

"Wow, that's an upscale place. How could Holly afford to live there? I thought she was an esthetician at a downtown spa."

"Yes, that is a problem, isn't it?"

"Ah, so you already knew she was living beyond her means."

"Perhaps she was looking after the apartment for someone."

"You might not like what you find. You better be prepared for that, Aunt Kay."

She folded the paper and put it in her purse. "Not knowing is always worse than finding out the truth. After we go to the apartment we have to locate the people who worked with Holly. Those are the ones who'll know what happened to her after she left Jacaranda."

"You've really thought this through, haven't you?"

"It was a long drive back from Sarasota."

"And do you think Holly's death has something to do with Angel disappearing?"

"I don't know." It was the shift in her eyes that told me she was lying.

CHAPTER 7

The parking area at the Sunset was nearly empty but across the road the public lot on the beach was quite busy. Hopefully a few of them would come in for lunch. I wouldn't even insist on shoes and a cover-up. The fear of impoverishment was making me real tolerant.

The Sunset is on the second floor of an old hotel with a panoramic view over the beach to the Gulf of Mexico. There's a tiny elevator that takes customers up to the dining room in what was once the ballroom with an outdoor porch. It's the best place on the whole West Coast of Florida to watch the sunset. And that's not just me bragging but an actual quote from a Florida living magazine review, which I framed and hung in the elevator.

I don't like elevators so I took the outside stairs at the north end. As I stepped through the door into the foyer my cell rang.

I opened the glass door to the bar, once a private club and my favorite part of the Sunset, as I answered the call. In the bar soft blues played in the background and huge ceiling fans, still run by the original pulley system, stirred air smelling of expensive perfume and very old scotch.

Clay said, "Hello, darlin'."

A tingle of desire ran down my spine . . . well, at least somewhere in that direction. A man who could lead a saint down the road to perdition and have her saying, "Thank you, Lord," when she got there, Clay could pretty much set everything on me vibrating.

But even as his velvet tones caressed me and turned my insides to jelly, his next words froze my heart.

"Sorry, babe, I've got bad news."

"Well, tell me quick so I can get straight to calling you a bastard."

There had been too many last-minute cancellations, so many missed dinners that our long-distance romance was surviving on memories alone. But I was crazy enough about Clay to put up with just about anything, including neglect.

"I can't make it home."

"Bastard."

"The guys from North Star Construction are coming in tonight to look over the project and they want a meeting first thing tomorrow."

"Will you be home after the meeting?"

"Only if it doesn't go well."

"And if it goes well?"

"I'll be home next weekend for sure."

I bit back sharp words while my brain called me a fool. I've got a real bad habit of hanging in too long, long after the party is over, and maybe I was doing it again hoping things would get better.

He sighed.

That sound set my heart fluttering. What hope did I have if just the sound of his sigh could warm me up enough to shed my clothes . . . along with my already very low standards? A kiss and I'd forgive him anything.

"I can't stand it," he said. "One way or another I'll be home in a week."

One more deadline, one more line in the sand.

What with the story about Holly, Isaak leaving me and Clay not coming home, I'd had all the bad news I could handle, but my already miserable day was about to get worse. Her name was Nora Simpson and she was one of Jacaranda's gentry. With two friends in tow, she walked into the foyer where I was standing in for the hostess. She smiled at me like she had a bug in her sights and was about to stick a pin through it. My worry meter cranked up to the danger zone.

Nora was Laura Kemp's best friend and Laura was Clay's ex-girlfriend, the woman everyone was expecting Clay to go back to the minute he came to his senses and dumped me.

Laura's clique never set foot in the Sunset so just coming through the door meant Nora Simpson was there for a purpose—and it wasn't to make my day better.

"How lovely to see you, Sherri."

"Likewise." My mouth stretched in an imitation of a smile every bit as sincere as hers.

She jutted a hip and looked me up and down. "I must say you're taking it well."

Having no idea what she was talking about, I gave a slight lift of my shoulder and said, "No problem."

"Really?" It was a long-drawn-out mocking sound. "I thought Laura being in Cedar Key with Clay would be a big problem for you."

I picked up three menus. "A table for three, is it?"

Nora glanced into the restaurant. "And that's not a problem either, I see." She gave me another faux smile. "I'm so happy you've managed to stay in business. I'm sure this is a terrible time for you, but then breakups aren't good at anytime, are they?"

I bit back, "You should know, bitch." No way was I going to drive away customers. She could dump on me all she wanted as long as she paid the bill, so I refrained from telling her that her own husband was having an affair with one of the ladies she was lunching with.

I tried another smile and said, "This way." I led them to a spot by the windows and set the menus down on a table with a pillar blocking the view. "Enjoy your lunch, ladies."

I walked away with my head high, telling myself if Laura was in Cedar Key there was a perfectly reasonable explanation. Trouble was, I couldn't think of it.

My experience with men wasn't encouraging. Jimmy Travis, my no-good dead husband, hadn't kept his marriage vows long enough for the wedding bouquet to wilt. For Jimmy, cheating was just a game and one he played with great delight. But Clay wasn't like that. At least that's what I told myself over and over. Repetition didn't seem to make it truer.

Nora wasn't done wielding the knife. I had just hung up from taking a cancellation when she came out to the foyer on her way to the ladies room. She stopped in front of me and said, "Don't worry. I'm sure you'll land on your feet, or in your case, your back."

"Thank you for your confidence in me." I turned away from her to greet two people getting off the elevator.

After I seated the new arrivals, I went into my office to make a call, intending to ask some pointed questions, like why is Laura Kemp in Cedar Key and is she the reason you can't make it home?

Clay and I are equal partners in the Sunset. If he wanted out of our relationship and our partnership—well, there was no use considering that situation. I sucked in some deep breaths, telling myself, "Don't start screaming before you know there's a fire."

When Clay finally picked up I gave him the good news, telling him Aunt Kay was making our late mortgage payments. "This will keep us alive until Thanksgiving."

"But I don't understand what she wants from you."

"She just wants me to drive her around a bit."

"It isn't dangerous, is it?"

"Naw. I'm going to drive her around and wait while she talks to people. I can carry on almost as if I was at the Sunset. Talking of dangerous, what is Laura Kemp doing in Cedar Key?"

The silence was so loud it was deafening. Clay said, "Don't go jumping to the wrong conclusions."

"I haven't jumped anything. I hope you can say the same." There was a choking sound but before he could yell I kept going. "And I haven't concluded anything except that the fact Laura Kemp is in Cedar Key hasn't gone unnoticed. People are starting to talk about us in the past tense."

His voice rose in protest, or maybe outrage. "She's decorating the model suite for me."

"Just make sure that's all she does for you."

"Are you jealous?"

"Why didn't you tell me she was going up there?"

"If you're not jealous, why do you care?"

Some truly rude comments came to mind. While I sorted through them for the most choice, Clay said, "Look, I didn't want to upset you."

I started to speak but he interrupted. "I know, I know, you couldn't care less, but still, you and Laura have a little history."

"A little history? More like our own civil war, not that it's ever been very civil."

"See what I mean? Just let it go. Laura's been great. She brought lots of her own stuff and has done a fantastic job. Plus, she's been helping to wine and dine these guys from the North who are going to save my bacon. And . . ."

"Stop," I shouted before he could sing any more of her praises. "She's so sweet I may throw up."

"See, there you go."

"You're right. Here I go." I hit End and then turned off my cell. It didn't matter. Clay wouldn't be calling back. Judging from past conversations like this it might be several days before one of us broke down and called.

Bugger! I wished I'd gotten some money out of Aunt Kay. Maybe I could talk her into paying half upfront. Then at least, if everything went for a dump, I'd have something. My mind played with the math. I could make a lot of suppliers happy and pay off a little on the mortgage. Maybe if I showed her I was trying I might be able to convince her to hand over a check.

I called Dan Raines. As I listened to the phone ringing, I worried that if Aunt Kay had time to think about her offer to me she'd change her mind. I should have gotten a check even if it was postdated.

"Hello," Shelly Raines said. I stumbled over telling Shelly my name and that I wanted to talk to Dan.

Dan's folks still lived in Jacaranda. They'd brought Shelly and Dan into the Sunset just the month before to celebrate Dan's birthday, but Dan and I hadn't really seen each other since high school.

"Dan worked the midnight shift," she said, easy and friendly and not at all curious why this woman she barely knew would want to come to her house and talk to her husband. "He's still sleeping. Come by about eight. Dan will be up by then."

CHAPTER 8

Gwen Morrison, our hostess, wasn't the only member of staff who wasn't available that Sunday night. My bartender also didn't make it in. It's pretty sad when even the staff gives up on you, but to be fair there weren't enough people in the place to make it worth his time.

I slipped behind the bar and listened to the woes of the few drinkers who did show up. Sometimes I think the only thing that brings customers up in the little elevator is the lure of having someone to talk to when they get to the top. Maybe it's no more than my blank expression, which they mistake for rapt attention, but people seem to confide in me, to trust me enough to dump all over me. For that privilege they're willing to buy overpriced alcohol. Recently, though, I've thought about getting a sign that says DON'T TELL ME YOUR PROBLEMS OR I'LL BE FORCED TO RECIPROCATE, but I figure it wouldn't add much to the ambiance.

And most nights other people's mistakes and bad decisions make for great entertainment. Not that night. That night a worm of worry was eating its way through my heart. Just the thought of losing Clay made tears well up.

I slipped into the kitchen to check on Miguel, who was in charge while Isaak was away. Miguel had everything under control. I was about to leave the kitchen when I turned back and asked, "Do you remember a waitress named Holly Mitchell?"

He didn't look up from plating an order. "*Si*, pretty little thing." His hand made a round motion in front of his stomach. "Very pregnant last time I see her." He looked up. "Crazy to think of that one being a mother . . . she may forget to feed it." He put three finished plates onto the high counter in front of him and hit a pager to summon a waitperson.

"When was this, when did you see her when she was pregnant?"

He turned and gave orders to a helper before he considered my question. "We were in Sarasota for my niece's first communion, before Christmas." He turned away, a steaming pan already in his hand.

The bar had more lonely people in it than normal that night, all of them making me crazy. Brian Spears came in just in time to save my sanity. Before either of us spoke I took down a bottle of Famous Grouse and showed him the label. He nodded. When I set the scotch in front of him, he lifted his glass to me and offered his usual toast. "Success to temperance."

I picked up the glass I had beneath the counter. "And to abstinence."

His first sip was followed by a contented sound and then he said, "Wait until you hear this, Sherri. According to your Uncle Ziggy, your father has a new girlfriend."

"Well, that just proves hope never dies. I must take after my old man after all."

"I have to say, your family is definitely entertaining."

"We aim to please."

The cash register pinged. I read the bar order and opened a bottle of red wine and set it on a tray with four glasses. "All of us Jenkinses like to keep things interesting."

"You always do that." Brian was not only my lawyer but also a longtime friend. He knew all about my folks, the ins and outs of family relationships and—from Ziggy's fire to the attack on the ranch by the local crazy—he'd been involved in more than one of our disasters.

"So who is the new girlfriend?" Brian asked.

"If Uncle Ziggy doesn't know, I sure don't." I delivered the wine to the wait station and came back to lean on the bar in front of Brian. "Old fool. It's bound to end badly—finish with tears and restraining orders."

He took an appreciative sip and made sounds of joy before going on with his story. "It's become some kind of a game for those two old buzzards. Ziggy's taken to sneaking up on Tully to figure out who it is your dad phones behind closed doors. Ziggy says it's definitely someone in Jacaranda so it must be someone we know."

"Probably a married woman," I said. "Dad likes it that way—they don't get ideas."

"Ziggy tried tailing him into town but Tully cottoned on to him, turning off his headlights and tearing off down a dirt road. They played tag in the dark like teenagers before Ziggy lost him."

Brian was grinning like a fool as he tipped his glass at me. "You are a shining member of one crazy clan."

"Show a little respect. It took two hundred years of inbreeding to arrive at our level of stupidity."

Brian jerked a thumb over his shoulder in the direction of the dining room. "I think it's one of your waitresses. Your dad took a keen interest in Maria at his birthday dinner."

"My father takes a keen interest in any female who comes within sniffing distance. It was about the only thing my parents had in common, an overwhelming interest in the opposite sex. It kept their lives interesting, deciding which one was currently misbehaving."

Brian lowered the glass halfway to his lips. "Do you suppose Ruth

Ann is back in town?" He answered his own question. "No, we'd all know if your mother was back. So who is it?"

"Why would I know, or care? My dad's life is his problem. I have enough troubles of my own."

CHAPTER 9

Dan Raines and his wife, Shelly, lived at the south end of Sarasota, about forty-five minutes north of Jacaranda.

Dan was already in his police uniform when he opened the door. He was overly cheerful but his eyes were wary. He tried to pretend that it was completely normal for me to knock on his door at quarter after eight on a Sunday night, only hours after he found the body of someone we both knew, something we didn't mention in front of Shelly.

After Dan and Shelly showed me around their new townhome and I cooed over Hannah, Shelly went off to put their baby to bed. Dan and I went outside, taking drinks with us.

The patio was a boxlike enclosure about ten by ten and stuffed with plants hanging on the wooden fence, a glass table with four chairs and a colossal barbeque shoved up against the fence. The smell of charred steak still lingered in the air.

As a kid, Dan Raines had been what you might call plump. Kids, not so nice, called him fat up until he was about twelve. That's when a big change happened to Dan. Around puberty the plumpness turned to muscle and the fireplug of a boy turned into a running back. It was the making of Dan. In high school, shining on both the football and wrestling teams, Dan went all the way to the state championships, and his self-confidence reflected his success.

Now, sitting across from me, Dan looked like a guy meant to be in uniform. His thick auburn hair was cut short and his square jaw was clean shaven. Everything about his appearance said upright and dependable, a man you could trust with your life.

The air conditioner hummed beside us but still I glanced up the side of the house to make sure all the windows were closed against the sweltering night. I didn't want Shelly to overhear Dan and me talking about Holly.

I watched Dan's face for a reaction and said, "Holly Mitchell is dead."

Dan sat up straighter. "Really? I'm sorry to hear it."

"Comes as a surprise to you, does it?"

"Well, yes, of course. What happened?"

"It seems she committed suicide."

"Too bad." He frowned. "She was usually pretty happy when she was a kid, although given the kind of person she became, perhaps it isn't unexpected."

"Why? What had she become? What was there about her that would lead to this?"

"She was a dipstick." Dan ran a hand over the kinked remnants of his curls. "She never stopped dreaming, never faced reality. How did she get like that?"

"How did you get to be a cop?"

Dan gave a soft snort of amusement, or perhaps disgust. "I never meant to be a cop. I was headed for law school, but I didn't like being caged in an office with books all day. I wanted action." With a wry smile he said, "It turns out policing is more like being a babysitter for adults who make really dumb choices. I thought it would be more about figuring out things and helping people, but it's more like telling a drunk, 'No, sir, you can't piss in that fountain,' or, 'No, lady, you can't drive on the sidewalk.' Adults doing really stupid things make up 95 per cent of my job."

"Mine too."

He grinned. Then he said, "How can Holly be dead?"

Dan wasn't really expecting an answer. It was more like he was exploring the whole idea of Holly being lifeless. He planted his forearms on his thighs and clasped his hands between his knees, studying the concrete slabs beneath his feet.

I waited.

Finally he lifted his head and said, "Did you drive all the way up from Jac just to tell me Holly is gone?"

"Yeah, that's about it." I took a sip of my beer. "There's a big difference in age between you and Holly, nearly ten years. How come you knew her so well?"

"We lived next door to each other. Back then the grade school kids and the high school kids took the same school bus." He pushed the soda can away from him. "Remember? We all rode together in the same white-roofed bus going over the north bridge to school in Jacaranda. Coming home, Holly and I both got off at the corner before you."

His handsome face screwed up in some kind of emotion I couldn't read. "She always wanted to walk home with me but I'd run ahead. I hated it when she spoke to me on the bus. It was embarrassing. I got teased for it. I told her over and over not to talk to me. I was kinda mean to her."

As I remembered it, I'd treated Dan just about the same. A year or two younger than me, in high school I never wanted to hang out with him or even acknowledge him in the halls. He was just a kid, a nuisance with all his eager enthusiasm.

"So you didn't expect this from Holly?" I reached out and touched the drop of condensation sliding down my beer bottle. "Expect her to kill herself?"

He shook his head slowly. "She was always so optimistic, absolutely convinced that things were about to be wonderful."

"I could use a little of that. These days, I tend to expect the worst." I tilted up the Budweiser and then asked, "When did you see her last?"

He shrugged. "It's been ages."

"Aunt Kay said Holly was crazy about you and always kept in touch."

He glanced up at me and frowned. "Not so much anymore, not since I got married."

"Didn't Shelly like it? I mean, didn't Shelly like you hanging out with Holly?"

"I didn't hang with Holly, and 'sides it has nothing to do with Shelly." His voice was sharp. "The last time we saw Holly she had purple hair and was strung out on something. Shelly pretty much felt sorry for Holly the few times they met."

"So when was that, when did you see her last?"

"About a year ago. Like I said, I haven't really seen her since I got married." Dan was brushing off my idle questions with answers he hadn't really thought out. He had been married pretty close to three years, but I didn't bother pointing out this disconnect in his story.

If he'd been the one to find Holly's dead body, he was over it. Or maybe there was another reason he was distancing himself from Holly.

I set the bottle on the table. "Don't shit me, Dan. The cops told Aunt Kay that an Officer Raines was first on the scene and found the body. You knew she was dead before I showed up on your doorstep."

He opened his mouth to deny it, but read my face and thought better of it. "Don't tell. I don't want it to come out that I was any more than the cop on duty when the call came in. There's no need for anyone to know."

"What don't you want people to know, that you were bonking her, or that you had something to do with her death?"

"Shit, Sherri." His fist slammed the glass table. I reached out and caught my beer before it could fall. He looked around, afraid someone might overhear. He looked up at the house and then stood up to check that his neighbors weren't outside. When he swung back to face me I could see the violence in him as he fought for control and searched for a lie.

"No matter what you come up with I'm not going to buy it," I said. "You had an affair with Holly. What was she, nineteen . . . twenty?"

His mouth was an angry slit and his jawbone worked under his skin. "It wasn't like that."

"No? What was it like? Did you push her around, beat her up? Aunt Kay said someone hurt her."

"It wasn't me. Christ, how could you think that?"

"So tell me what it was like, Dan."

"It was stupid." He breathed deeply and let it out slowly, forcing himself to calm down. "She was always so eager, so wanting to please, so . . ." He looked away. "It only lasted for a few weeks and then I found out that Shelly was pregnant. I really wanted a kid. We've been trying since we got married. Shelly went for tests and we knew it might not happen. But then she was pregnant. We were so happy."

"Tell me about Holly."

"I told Holly it was over. The thing with Holly didn't mean anything."

Those were the words Jimmy always used when he begged me to take him back. "I'm sure it meant something to Holly."

He ran the back of his hand across his mouth. "She took it hard. I had to tell her again and again to stop calling and leaving me messages. Once, I came off shift and found a pink note stuck under my wiper blades. She just didn't give up, didn't get it. We were over. I never saw her again after the day I told her it was done."

"You mean you never saw her again while she was alive. Why didn't you identify Holly instead of leaving it up to Aunt Kay? You could've done that without telling the cops anything more."

"I panicked. I can't afford to be associated with Holly." He leaned forward. "I could see bruising on her face. Someone had worked her over. She'd lost weight, didn't look good. I think she'd really had a hard time of it in this last year."

I waited.

"There's something else. Don't tell anyone, will you?"

"No," I lied.

CHAPTER 10

"Her cell was there on the table. I checked it. It had some messages on it."

He glanced at the house before he told me his ugly news. "They called back several times, getting more pissed with her each time. The messages were reminding her of a date. I checked the number. It was an escort service."

Dan picked up his soda and set it down again. "It wouldn't do my career any good if my superiors found out I'd been involved with a sex worker. That's why I couldn't identify her."

"Was she a sex worker before she slept with you, or is that what you turned her into?"

"This has nothing to do with me." His voice was too loud. He lowered his voice. "It was long done between us. Whatever she became, however she died, it has nothing to do with me."

"For god's sake, you could have at least admitted you knew her. I wasn't expecting you to tell anyone you screwed her. Instead you left it to a sick old woman to go to the morgue and identify her."

"I'm sorry."

He sounded like a petulant little boy, more worried about being in trouble than if he hurt someone.

"Tell it to Aunt Kay."

We stayed silent for the length of time it took me to drink the second half of my beer and then I asked, "Was that how she was found? Did the escort service call the police?"

He looked down at the patio stones. "Maybe. I was only told an anonymous call was made. I was the patrol in the area so I was sent to check it out. The super let me in."

"Wasn't that an interesting fluke? Officer Raines was the uniform on duty, the cop called to check out Holly's apartment."

"Things like that happen. I've been sent twice to accidents where I knew people."

"Yeah? Well, I stopped believing in coincidences when I found my Christmas presents under my mother's bed, the same ones that were wrapped and under the tree from Santa on Christmas morning."

The angry silence stretched between us. Finally, I said, "Was anyone else living in the apartment?"

"No sign of it."

"So what's the name of this escort service?"

"Why?" He straightened. "Stay out of this. It's none of your business." He was a cop again and taking control.

"Okay." I changed the subject. "It's hard to believe, hard to get your head around. Not only that Holly is dead, but that this is what she became. She was always so sweet, even with the nastiest, hardest-to-please diners. Aunt Kay said she wanted to be an actress or a model from the time she was a little girl."

He met my eyes now. "Maybe that's why she killed herself. Maybe she quit believing in her dreams."

"They showed Aunt Kay her note."

"We always show the family the suicide note. It helps them understand, or maybe it's just to convince them it happened, and we need them to identify the handwriting."

I got a pen and a piece of paper out of my purse. "Write down her words, just like in the note."

He started to argue.

"I can always call and request it."

"They won't tell you."

"Maybe not, but I've got such a big mouth, you never know what will slip out."

His jaw hardened and tiny bulges jumped in his cheek. It was touch and go if he was going to throw me out or do as I asked. He picked up the pen and pulled the paper towards him and wrote quickly.

He shoved it back at me and I read,

> because my Angel is gone and I can't live without my Angel. I have no home and no one to look after me. I have nothing left. This is the only way.

It was signed, "Love, Holly."

"Was this what it said?"

"Exactly. It's precisely the same as her note. You might not realize it, but I'm damn good at my job. I don't make mistakes."

I so wanted to point out the obvious exception.

"It's just that it's an odd note. The first word doesn't begin with a capital letter. Don't you think that's strange?"

"It's a suicide note, not an English essay."

"Still . . . things like that are habits. Holly was always meticulous about taking orders." Suddenly I was struck by a horrible idea. "Are you sure she committed suicide?"

His hand slammed on the glass table. "Don't go turning this into some big mystery. It isn't. She killed herself . . . end of story."

I shoved the paper and pen back into my purse and said, "Holly was okay, nice really, but sometimes she got on my nerves, always wanting to hang out after work. I was past girls like her."

Dan tilted back on his chair. "When we were kids we all wanted to be around you. You were always the one who started things, some-times trouble but always fun."

"Things change. I used to think I could handle anything. Not so much these days."

His chair thudded onto the concrete and he nodded in agree-ment. "That's how I felt until I found Holly. I thought I was immune to shock but seeing her . . ." He didn't finish.

Somewhere down the row of houses a door slammed and a voice called out a name.

I watched Dan closely. "Aunt Kay is convinced that Holly had a baby."

Dan's mouth gaped open. His spine straightened and he pushed back against the chair where he'd been lounging. "What? No, no way, she didn't have a baby." If he was lying, it was a damn good act.

"Aunt Kay says she did. She wants to know what happened to the baby."

"Well, she's wrong. There was no baby. It never happened."

I looked at the pile of wooden blocks sitting on the table. "How old is Hannah?"

He didn't answer.

I peeled the label off the damp bottle. "She's not a year yet, is she?" Still he didn't respond, couldn't even look at me.

"Holly must have got pregnant about the same time as Shelly."

"Oh, shit," he said.

"Did you know about Holly's baby?"

"God, no!"

I believed him, but he wouldn't be the first liar I'd believed.

He ran his hand over his head. "What makes Aunt Kay think Holly had a baby?" You could see he was hungry for it all to be a stupid mix-up. "She's old and she's got it wrong."

"Holly came by with the baby and wanted Aunt Kay to look after her."

"There was no sign of a baby in that apartment. I followed procedure and looked through every room to make sure there was no one else there, alive or dead. There was no sign of a kid. The apartment was totally clean and neat, like a model suite ready for a showing."

"Maybe someone should find out what happened to Holly's baby. Will you help me, Dan?"

"Shit, no, it has nothing to do with me."

We both knew he was wrong there.

"And you're sure Holly's death was a suicide?"

"You read the note. She'd lost her angels or something. You know what she was like. That's why I thought . . ." He ran his hands over his head. "I thought she'd finally come face to face with the truth. She was never going to be rich and famous."

Living without dreams, giving up on her dreams? It was possible.

"The note was written on pink notepaper and it had an empty highball glass sitting on it. I figure she washed down some pills with a strong drink."

"Was there an empty pill bottle?"

"Not that I saw, but I didn't check the garbage. That's up to the investigators. The autopsy will tell what she used."

"Can you get the autopsy results?"

"Why?" He looked at me warily. "Why do you want to know how she died?"

"Idle curiosity."

"Curiosity killed the cat."

"Is that a threat?"

"Why would I threaten you?"

Why indeed? One more thing was worrying me. "Dan, if Holly called you before she died, if you made an anonymous call, knowing you'd be the one who would be sent to check her out, your cell phone number is on her phone. You can't hide from that."

He stared at me without answering.

"But of course you wouldn't be that stupid. You'd have used a payphone. Or maybe you have a throwaway."

He looked up at the sky that was alive with color from the dying sun. "Remember the night we all went skinny dipping out at Rum Bay? Nights like that, when you wanted to stop time and just stay where you were forever—how come we don't have nights like that anymore, Sherri? When did life get so serious?"

"Maybe that's what happens when you grow up."

CHAPTER 11

On the drive back to Jac, I tried to decide how honest Dan had been with me and what he had left out of the story. Dan was quick to anger, always had been; could that anger get out of control if his family was threatened? Holly and a baby could definitely stick a pin in his happy family bubble.

There were more questions bumping into each other in my brain. Had he known Holly was dead before he went to that apartment? I only thought of that one when I hit the ramp to the I-95 but I kept coming back to the biggest question of all. Did Dan know where Holly's baby was? Hannah and Angel would be about the same age. Maybe Angel was hiding in plain sight. Maybe I'd already found Angel.

At the borrowed beach house I turned on an antiquated computer that the owners had left behind. Surfing the back alleys of the Internet and delving into the seedy side of paradise, I went through half a dozen Sarasota escort services before I found Holly at the Angel Escort Agency. On the screen she was no longer the woman I remembered, bubbling and alive. She'd been turned into a lifeless mannequin, a plaything for perverts.

The pictures were lewd but artful in their use of setting and lighting to create a mood and tell a story. Each woman on the site seemed to be speaking to a particular fantasy, from violence and domination to extreme vulnerability. That's where Holly fit in. Pale and terrified, she was wearing a white thong and thigh-high white stockings with gold spiked heels. Sprawled on a bed with her wrists tied, a discarded girl-child, looking at least five or more years younger than her actual age, she was begging the camera for mercy while waiting for the blow that would end it all.

In another picture she was tied to a chair with her legs spread to the camera. The look on her face was one of sheer panic, a victim waiting to be violated.

"Oh, Holly, what happened to you?" This wasn't the magenta-haired laughing girl I'd known.

Holly had been turned into a victim. All of the shots of her were designed to appeal to the most base and depraved cravings of men. I felt sullied and corrupted just by looking at those images, complicit in her abuse. How do escort services get away with putting up these websites, advertising human flesh for sale with the prices laid right out there?

I searched for more information about Angel Escort Agency, but all I came up with was Angel Photography. According to the site, they did "Intimate pictures for the one you love." The quality of the sample pictures showed the same talent as those on the escort website.

Angel Photography Studios also shot portfolios for models. Had Holly started out getting pictures taken for her modeling career and ended up in the escort trade? It bothered me that the name of Holly's baby was the same as that of the escort service. That was just wrong, but maybe it would tell me something about Angel I needed to know.

I wrote down the telephone numbers for the photo studio and the escort agency and tucked them into my pocketbook. At least I would have something to show Aunt Kay before I asked her for money.

I checked my voicemail. At ten o'clock Clay had called to say goodnight. I tried his cell but it went directly to voicemail. I didn't leave a message.

CHAPTER 12

Sleep was fleeting. By six o'clock on Monday morning I called it quits and went for a run on the beach. The crimson sky was opening like a flower above me and tiny birds ran ahead of me in the foam at the edge of the surf. Except for the brash call of gulls and the lap of waves, the beach was quiet, not another human in sight. The salt-laden air was more of a caress than the heavy blanket of heat and humidity it would be later in the day.

The tide was out. The broad, hard-packed sand at the edge of the waves was perfect to run on, although it turned out to be a lot more like a bit of running with a lot of puffing and walking in between. It didn't matter. I was in the place I loved best. I focused on the soft squish of my trainers in the sand, letting the rhythm hypnotize me into the moment.

By the time I got back to the cottage I was sweating and exhausted. I turned on the radio while I drank the last of the orange juice from the carton. The weatherman predicted another scorcher and talked about a tropical storm headed our way from Africa. It had the potential of becoming a hurricane.

Hurricanes need warm water to feed on. With the waters surrounding Florida hotter than normal, the hurricane season was going to extend far into November, another reason besides the economy for visitors to stay away. I switched off the radio.

There was no hurricane insurance on the Sunset. We call it self-insuring down here in Florida, which really means, "I've got my ass hung out way over the line."

In the drab bathroom, where mold grew and the blistered ceiling dropped paint flakes, I caught sight of myself in the mirror. I was wearing a tee-shirt, oversized, graying and ugly, which likely went back to my days with Jimmy. The top was matched with a pair of men's boxer shorts with golf balls on them that I'd given to Clay for Christmas. I thought they were cute, but he'd refused to wear them so I did. When had I started dressing like this? Not pretty and not enticing. Maybe it was my own fault that Clay didn't come home.

I noticed something else. I pulled the tee-shirt up tight around my waist and chest, bunched it all up in back and held it in a knot. Those ten extra pounds that happiness and living with Clay had put on had been taken off by anxiety and loneliness, the upside to bankruptcy.

My hair was caught up in a twist and nailed to the top of my head by a clasp. I let it down and squeezed up my face in disgust. My hair was mousy. No other word for it. I'd noticed months ago that it wasn't looking its best and I'd even bought a box of color. It was still there under the sink.

Before I went anywhere I was going to shine this girl up. As Ruth Ann always said, "There's no use feeling bad and looking bad too."

An hour later I checked myself out in that same mirror. "Welcome back." In the mirror, the new Sherri's hair shone darkly and her nails were gleaming China Red.

My cell rang.

"Hi, Clay." And even before he could answer I asked, "Are you coming home?"

"Not yet. The meeting went well and we're still talking."

I tried real hard to believe that was the only reason he wasn't speeding south towards me.

There was another option. The highway ran both ways. But Aunt Kay's money was the difference between keeping the Sunset and losing it. Those three months' worth of grace kept me from packing.

Aunt Kay had moved out east of Tamiami Trail into a nice subdivision full of entry-level computer programmers, retired folks and self-employed tradesmen. The two-bedroom ranchers were built of cement blocks set on a slab of concrete. Each lot had a solitary citrus tree set in a precision-cut front yard.

I'm still a trailer tramp at heart, and the suburbs throw me into a panic, set me gasping for breath and looking for a line of attack to smash my way out. The neatness and sameness of this neighborhood had me hungering to see a house painted pink with purple trim in a rugged show of individualism.

Aunt Kay answered her door and left it open for me while she went to get her handbag off the kitchen table. She took out an envelope and handed it to me. "This is for you."

I opened the envelope and checked the date. Like she'd warned me, the check was postdated to Saturday. "Look, maybe we could make a deal. How be you pay me half now and the other half on Saturday."

"Nope."

"Well, maybe we should go day by day."

"Nope."

"Why?"

"I want you as interested in finding Angel as I am. Money is a great motivator." She pointed a finger at me. "And trust me on this . . . If you don't put your all into this, I'll cancel the check."

I opened my mouth to argue, but her locked-down face plus past experience told me to save my breath. I'd only make the situation worse. I put the check away.

"I talked to Dan Raines."

Her face lit with excitement. "Tell me everything." She pulled out a chair and sat down at the kitchen table.

I did as ordered. Well, most of it. I told her that Dan likely was Angel's father and that he was the one to find Holly. I didn't tell her how Holly was earning her money, didn't tell her about the pictures. I still had this feeling that I should shield her from such harsh realities. In truth, she needed protecting about as much as a rabid Rottweiler did.

Aunt Kay asked most of the questions I'd asked myself the night before. After I'd told her a half-dozen times that I didn't know the answer to the questions she was asking, she got to her feet and said, "Okay, let's go to Sarasota, go see where she died." She slid the strap of her oversized handbag over her arm and waved me towards the door.

We weren't even out the door before she stopped dead in her tracks. "I also need to see Dan's baby. Maybe Hannah and Angel are the same child. Maybe Holly turned Angel over to her father."

"People would know if Shelly was pregnant. Or do you think she faked a pregnancy?"

"If she did it would only be for a few months, or maybe it was handled like any adoption. It's even possible that the adoption is no secret."

She thought for a moment. "I'll decide when I see the baby if it's Angel."

"Would you recognize Angel after all these months?"

"I'm not sure."

I pulled my phone out and showed her the picture I'd taken the night before.

Aunt Kay studied the image a long time before she sighed and said, "I'm not sure. I have to see her in person."

"Shelly and Hannah are in Orlando visiting her sister until Friday;

besides, it's been months and babies change. Let's see if anything else turns up before we go bothering Dan's family."

"Credit me with a little sense."

I bit back a retort and opened the door to the truck for her. The check I had tucked into my shoulder bag was making me more patient than I normally would be.

She put her left foot in and then attempted to hoist her hip up onto the seat. She was too short. We'd gone through this the day before when I brought her home. I should have remembered and gotten a box for her to stand on.

I looked around but couldn't see anything that would help. Now, there's where the trailer park has it all over the burbs. Back at the edge of the swamp there was so much junk lying around, I could have built a ramp for a rocket.

She managed to get her left hip up near the seat but she just wasn't making it on her own. I planted both hands under her rear end and heaved. It did the trick.

Aunt Kay laughed. "I'm really not that kind of a girl, but thanks for the lift."

"It may not be elegant but it worked."

"Yes, but people will talk."

I drove out to Tamiami Trail and headed north with Aunt Kay beside me, humming softly away to herself, and the hot road shimmering in front of me. Even if she hadn't been paying me to chauffeur her around, the drive would be worth it just to see her happy.

CHAPTER 13

Sarasota is a gorgeous city south of Tampa on the Gulf of Mexico. With long arching bridges going out to Siesta Key and Longboat Key, it has some of the finest white sand beaches in the world. And for the tourists who don't drool over Sarasota's beaches and azure waters, there are historic areas, little pockets of lush tropical plantings with brick courtyards, art studios and restaurants. Best of all, Sarasota is only a short drive north of Jac, for when we want a taste of something more sophisticated than our own little Eden offers.

Holly's building was a surprise—a glamorous structure about nine stories tall with a green copper roof perched on top like a Chinese hat. A smaller pergola-like arrangement, stretched across the front entrance, had a matching roof. The landscaping was elaborate. Bird of paradise and hibiscus surrounded a fountain shooting water twelve feet into the air. On either side of the entrance was a raked Japanese garden.

It all said money.

I pulled up under the overhang and leaned towards the windshield, straining for a better view of the building. "I live with a real estate guy. I bet the one-bedroom condos here, even in this economy, are likely three-quarters of a million."

"Perhaps Holly had a second job."

What Holly was doing wasn't a job, more like the oldest profession.

"Maybe she had a roommate." Aunt Kay was still trying to put a shine on an apple with a worm in it.

"Even with more than one roommate she couldn't pay the condo fees on this place."

"Maybe she finally had some success." She gave a weary sigh. The ugly truth was right in front of her face and hard to ignore.

I said, "How are we going to get in?"

"There are advantages to being old and harmless. I'll get in and then I'll let you in."

"Oh, really? Okay, Houdini, this I got to see."

Aunt Kay held onto the top of the door and slid off the seat to the ground. "Don't be long," she said. The door slammed.

I went to look for the visitor parking area, expecting her to be right where I'd left her when I returned.

I strolled back to the front of the building. The heat was already making my tee-shirt stick to me but it would be even worse for Aunt Kay. I calculated how soon she would tire of this and want to go home. It was going to be easy money.

At the entrance I saw her hurrying to the front door ahead of a well-dressed man. Hunting in her purse for something, she appeared totally confused and demented. She was mumbling, "Where is it?" The man swiped a card key over a black pad and opened the door, holding it nicely for Aunt Kay to enter.

"Oh, thank you, dear," she said giving him a grateful smile.

He returned her smile, a beam that said, "Poor old thing, she's just like Grandma." Inside, Aunt Kay moved slowly, still searching in her purse while the man walked ahead to the elevators, already forgetting her.

When he was out of sight, Aunt Kay hurried back to open the door for me.

"Nice," I said.

Inside, the lobby was welcomingly chilled and smelled of cleaning solution.

I peeked down the hall to the elevators. "Now we're inside what good does it do?"

"I don't know. We'll have to figure out how to get up to Holly's apartment. I watched that man. You need one of those credit-card keys to work the elevators."

"Even if we get up to her floor, we can't get into her apartment without a key. And won't the police have it sealed?"

She considered it for a minute. "I don't know that either."

"Well, that's the way it happens on TV. The scene of a death is sealed off until they decide what really happened."

"But they already know what happened. She killed herself." She looked at me, confusion and despair on her face. "I thought being here would help us in some way. I didn't think it out too well, did I?"

I rubbed my arms. The lobby, which had felt cool when I entered, was actually frigid. "Perhaps we should go."

The sound of a door closing down the corridor to our right set Aunt Kay digging in her purse again.

I distanced myself from her, checking for missed calls and trying to look as if I was waiting for someone.

I stole a glance at the person coming towards us. Mid-forties female, wearing a shapeless sweater over tan slacks and a black tee-shirt, her black bedroom slippers made slapping noises on the travertine.

Apparently Aunt Kay decided that this was the sort of person she needed. She looked up and smiled, addle-brained and feeble. "Excuse me. Could you help me?"

The woman took her hands out of the sweater's pockets. Her voice was cross. She looked from Aunt Kay to me, but I already had my cell up to my ear as if I was listening.

The big woman, at least five foot ten with bones well covered with flesh, turned back to Aunt Kay. "How did you get into the building?" Aunt Kay was about to be shown the door.

"Oh, dear," Aunt Kay said and sighed. Her hand fluttered and then she pressed her fingers to her lips. "So foolish." Aunt Kay sank to a gilt chair standing by a glass console table. Her whole body seemed to wilt. I almost felt sorry for her myself.

"Can I help you?" the woman asked, right on cue.

"Oh, yes, I hope you can. I can't find my niece's address. Oh dear, so silly of me, I hope I haven't left my address book on the kitchen table. You see, I got it out to check the address." Aunt Kay's hand fluttered in the air about her head. "I get so confused." She went back to sorting through the jumble of her purse, taking things out and dropping them in her lap and onto the floor before retrieving some and stuffing them into her purse again. "I just can't believe I could be so stupid." Aunt Kay's voice trembled.

The woman bent over and gathered wayward items from the floor. "It's all right," she said, handing back Aunt Kay's things.

"I guess my children are right, I'm losing it. That's what they keep saying, over and over. Whatever am I going to do now?" Her shoulders shuddered.

The woman's voice was gentle when she asked, "Who's your niece?"

"Holly, Holly Mitchell." Aunt Kay looked up, all brightly eager and hopeful. "Do you know her?"

The woman's mouth opened and closed. She turned her body slightly away from Aunt Kay, saying, "Better come with me." The woman pointed down the corridor. "I'll make you a cup of tea. I'm the super here. My name is Bella Gornoy." She tucked her hair behind her ears. "It's just down here." She took a few steps down the hall.

"Oh, how kind." Aunt Kay pushed herself upright and limped after the woman. "That's just what I need, a cup of tea."

I went outside to wait for Aunt Kay to return or for the cops to come and pick her up. Either way, I wasn't going to be caught inside the building. Aunt Kay was on her own.

CHAPTER 14

I sat on a stone bench in the shade, happy to shake free of Aunt Kay and her plans so I could make some calls. Driving her around was going to work fine. I could take her where she wanted to go and while she played detective, I could run the Sunset.

I pulled my phone out and caught up, straightening out some scheduling problems and calling my wine merchant.

I still had some calls to make, but the air smelled of jasmine. Somewhere near my head a bee buzzed . . . wind chimes tinkled gently . . . Not even worry could stop my head from drooping. I closed my eyes, letting the sleepless night catch up.

My cell played "Dixie" and I jerked awake.

"You are not going to frigging believe this," a voice said.

"These days I could believe anything, including, 'The end is nigh.' I can really believe that one."

"Parrots," Gwen Morrison said. "The palms outside the dining-room windows are full of parrots. People are coming upstairs just to get a better look at them."

"And this is good because . . . ?"

"Because, Oh Thick One, these people may stay for lunch. I've called the radio station and the newspaper. It's been on the radio already."

Parrots don't belong in Florida. We have a big problem here with exotic species running loose, from boa constrictors eating alligators to chimps terrorizing whole neighborhoods up in Tampa. Down in the Everglades they've even opened a hunting season for pythons. Tens of thousands of pythons are slithering about the Everglades eating the native birds and mammals. At over twenty feet long and up to two hundred pounds, a snake that can both climb and swim . . . well, let's just say camping in the reeds isn't going to be my kind of fun anytime soon. But a whole lot of crazy men I know think it sounds like a high old time to go down there and have a go at snake hunting. They've already applied for licenses. Those guys will probably kill more hunters than pythons.

"Can you imagine? Parrots! Isn't that great?" Gwen said.

"Great hardly covers it! We don't want them flying away until at least after the dinner hour. How can we keep the little buggers there, nail them to the branches?"

"The humane society may frown on that tactic."

"Okay, cover the branches with peanut butter."

"The Chamber of Commerce may frown on that."

"Screw them. They aren't running a restaurant and trying to stay alive in this economy."

"Well, let's just hope these birds hang around for a day or two, with or without any help from you. In the meantime, I'll spread some peanuts under the trees and pretend it was one more stupid tourist who did it. Man, how do people get by without tourists to blame things on?"

"Blame it on staff like I'm going to if this goes wrong."

"You better get your ass back here. I don't want to call in extra servers."

"I'll be there soon. By the way, do you remember Holly Mitchell?"

"Of course. Flighty, pretty little thing, who was going to be in movies and was only at the Sunset while she waited for her big break. The worst waitress we ever had."

"That's her."

I told Gwen that Holly had committed suicide. She said, "I can't believe it. It just doesn't seem possible."

Sitting there, looking at a little garden of sand and rocks with miniature stone temples, I agreed—it wasn't feasible. "Do you remember anything else about her?"

"Only that Zach Maguire became our best customer when she was here."

"Zach?"

"Yeah, you remember. He always sat right by the waitress's station, where they pick up the drink orders, and talked to Holly. I remember you were about to toss his ass out of there because he slowed her down, but she dumped him before you got around to it."

"That's right. He works at my bank. I think he's the loan manager or something because he called about my overdraft. I should have tossed him out while I had the chance. Do you know that the Bank of America in Jacaranda frowns on you not paying something on your overdraft every month?"

"How mean-spirited of them!"

"I wonder if Zach has any discretion on when they call in my loan."

"If he does, I suggest you put on one of your Sherri-the-Slut outfits and go make nice with Zach."

"I'll wear red heels. Not a man alive can say no to a woman wearing red stilettos."

"They're susceptible to those as well," she agreed.

"You realize, of course, that this goes strictly against Clay's advice on how to do business."

"Yeah? Well, you and I both know how the real business is done. And would you rather drown wearing red stilettos or sensible pumps?"

"Wearing red all the way . . . Of course, if this thing I'm working on turns out, I won't need to worry about the bank."

"Is this 'thing' legal?"

Before I could answer, Gwen said, "Scratch that question. I don't want to know."

"Wise, very wise."

I saw the woman in the long sweater walk Aunt Kay to the door. "Gotta go." I stood up and walked away, not wanting the woman to ask what I was still doing there. I waited out of sight for Aunt Kay. She was red-faced and puffing when she joined me.

"Slow down," I cautioned, suddenly remembering her heart condition. "Better still, wait right here and I'll bring the truck."

She shook her head. "Just give me your arm."

"This weather can't be good for you."

"It isn't the temperature; it's any exertion. I'm fine." She leaned on me and we ambled at tortoise speed to the truck with heat shimmering off the pavement like we were walking through fire and breathing air that smelled scorched and dusty.

"It was very interesting." Aunt Kay stopped so she could talk and still breathe. "She did know Holly."

"Wait 'til we're in the truck." I didn't want her dying right there on the pavement.

At the passenger door we did another undignified heft of her behind to get her inside. She said, "If this intimate handling of my person goes on I expect you to at least buy me lunch."

"And I expect you to pay for my chiropractor."

She sat on the passenger seat, huffing and puffing, while I went around to the driver's side, which faced the sun. I cautiously tested the door handle. It was sizzling enough to sear a steak, so I bunched up my tee and used it to protect my hand. When I slipped behind the wheel, Aunt Kay had a little dollar-store fan out and was working it furiously. It took her some time before she was able to say, "Bella's little apartment was the cleanest home I ever saw. It was barren, it was so clean. No signs of living at all. It smelled like it had been disinfected."

I turned on the engine and rolled down the windows while I checked out Aunt Kay's color. She wasn't too pale anymore.

She stopped talking and sucked in several deep breaths, blowing air out slowly between pursed lips.

"I told her that I woke up this morning thinking of Holly and decided I'd take a chance on finding her in. I could see she was worried about how to tell me Holly was gone."

This was going to be a long story. I rolled my shoulders, stretched my neck from side to side and fought for patience.

"I felt badly about lying to her."

I reached in back of the passenger seat and took two bottles of water from my cooler.

"Did Bella know Holly?" I asked, thinking this might save about an hour and a half.

"Not really. Bella only knew Holly in the most casual way, said they talked while Bella cleaned the laundry room and Holly did her laundry." Aunt Kay's stories have a way of rambling. I unscrewed the top and handed her a bottle of water.

Aunt Kay held the bottle to the inside of her wrist. "Apparently people aren't supposed to just leave their laundry and go back upstairs."

"Just like they're not supposed to let strangers into the building."

"Yes, dear." She switched the bottle to her right wrist. "She made tea. On a day where we've already broken a record for morning temperature, she put the kettle on. People think that's what old ladies drink and that's what you do in a time of crisis. She told me Holly obeyed the rules, always stayed right there 'til her laundry was done.

Knowing Holly, it was probably more in the hopes of having company rather than respect for the rules. Holly hated being alone, never could play on her own." She turned her head to look at me. "Bella told me something else."

Aunt Kay took a tissue out of her purse and dabbed at the sweat on her face and neck. "Bella saw bruises on Holly's arms and even her upper chest, but her legs and the inside of her thighs had the heaviest marks." The tissue was worked into a small ball in Aunt Kay's fingers. "Seems Holly was beaten over a long period of time."

I cursed and then said, "Sorry."

"She didn't ask how Holly got them but I think Bella was hoping I'd tell her."

I took a deep breath and dived in. "Look, there are some things I have to tell you."

She turned to face me, already knowing she wasn't going to like what was coming.

"Holly was working for an escort service." I closed the windows and let the air conditioning take over. "I went online last night and searched through Sarasota escort services until I found her."

I studied Aunt Kay to see how she was taking this. "There are pictures of girls there, disgusting, and they tell . . . well, kinda what they're willing to do."

She nodded her head, looking worried but not shocked. "So that explains how she could afford that apartment."

"I don't think so." I studied the honey-colored wall I was parked in front of. "The prices were listed. She wouldn't make enough even as an escort."

Aunt Kay asked, "How do you explain the apartment?"

"I can't."

"And the bruising?"

"Maybe that was what Holly was willing to do."

"Oh."

"Has Bella seen the baby?"

"She didn't know anything about a baby. It's an adults-only building and in all the months Holly's been there, Bella didn't think Holly even had anyone visit with a baby. She said, 'Someone with a baby wouldn't be Holly's sort of friend,' then she remembered who she was talking to and snapped her mouth closed pretty quick. It was as if she were holding back all kinds of things an aunt might not want to hear." Aunt Kay's voice was filled with regret. "And Bella didn't know anyone named Denny or Danny and never saw a man in uniform in the building. I didn't say it was a man in a police uniform I was interested in."

"Did you get Bella's social security number?"

She turned to me, wide-eyed with surprise, "Why would I want that?"

I grinned. "I don't know, but it seems you got everything else."

"She did say she let the officer in on Saturday night."

"So Dan didn't have a key."

"Or he was too smart to use it. I told Bella that I was a little worried about Holly's finances; seeing the building and all . . . told her I was concerned Holly might be falling behind in her rent."

"What did Bella say to that?"

"She said most people pay directly from their bank or with post-dated checks. The super doesn't do the collecting now like they did when I lived in an apartment. So I asked if I could just wait in Holly's apartment until Holly came home."

"You were wasted on childcare. You should have been a cop."

"They're much the same thing some days. Bella told me Holly was away."

"If the baby has never been here, I don't suppose there's much to be gained by going into her apartment. Dan looked around and he didn't find anything."

"But he wasn't looking for signs of Angel. I thought I might find an address or a name, anything to tell us where the baby might be." Her hand curled into fists. "Where is Angel now and is she safe? That's what I keep asking myself."

"What are you going to do if we find the baby?"

She shrugged. "I just want to know that she is fine and then I'll let it go. I owe Holly that much."

But would she? Did Aunt Kay have some secret wish to have Angel for her own? Surely Aunt Kay was too old and too wise to daydream along those lines for long.

"What if the baby isn't fine?"

"We'll cross that bridge when we come to it." She looked away. "You don't think Holly would sell her child, do you Sherri?"

"Lord . . . where did that come from?"

"Holly was impractical and easily led." She turned back to me. "I believe she might convince herself that it was for the best and she was doing the right thing, even the best thing for Angel."

"But still . . ."

"This place says wealth," Aunt Kay said. "What else did she have to sell besides herself and her baby?"

"Evil never surprises you, does it?"

"It's just like any other human trait, like jealousy or hate or love." Aunt Kay waved a hand to the exit. "Let's see where Holly lived before she came here."

"Are you sure you're up to it?"

"What? Is it past my bedtime?"

"Okay, I was only asking." I backed out.

She pulled down the seat belt. "We need to find someone Holly talked to; she wouldn't be able to keep all of this to herself."

"It's probably a waste of time."

"Nevertheless, I've paid for a week of your time and paid well."

I held my tongue and tipped up the water bottle while I waited for traffic to clear.

Aunt Kay said, "We need to go to that escort agency."

I spewed water all over the windshield.

CHAPTER 15

"Escort services are really . . ." I searched for nice words. "Well, pretty much prostitution."

"Yes, I figured that out." Aunt Kay wiped her face and upper chest with a fresh tissue. "What's the name of this escort service?"

"Angel Escort Agency."

"Angel . . . You don't suppose . . . ?"

"That occurred to me."

She shook her head. "It doesn't seem possible but let's just go see them and find out what we can about Holly."

"There wasn't an address, just a telephone number."

She thought it over. "I guess they don't take walk-in customers. Just send girls out."

"There's no way to find them without an address."

Aunt Kay solved that problem in no time at all. "Call them and say you're looking for a job. They'll want to see you before they hire you. They'll need to tell you what to do and everything."

"You want me to pretend to be a prostitute?"

"No, no, just . . . well . . . I don't know. Just pretend to be interested. I'm going with you so it will be safe."

"Oh, that makes me feel loads better. And arriving at an interview for a job as a hooker, with my auntie by my side to protect me, will be a first for them. It'll have them rolling on the floor with laughter."

Switching gears, I said, "Let's tell the cops Holly had a baby. Where's that card the cop gave you? Let's call him now."

"Do you think they'll be interested in what happened to the baby if no crime has been committed? I tried yesterday to tell them about Angel. They're only making sure it was a suicide. After that they had no further interest in Holly."

"But pretending . . ."

"Please, Sherri."

"How many ways can this go wrong?"

"If you weren't going to go see them, why did you look them up on the Internet?"

"Curiosity."

"Pffft." It was a sound of absolute disbelief.

"Look, Aunt Kay, there's no doubt about what Holly was doing. The prices were there, by the hour or for all night. These aren't nice places."

"I'll try not to die from shock on you. It's the only way we can find out about that side of Holly's life."

She held out her hand. "Where's the number? I'll make the call if you can't."

"How do you know I have the number?"

"You looked it up, didn't you? Were you going there by yourself?"

"No way. I was going to give it to Dan."

"He already knew about the agency, had the number off of Holly's phone. You used to lie better."

After a minute she said, "Do you think he'll go check it out?"

"Nope."

"So, you were going there alone." She reached over and patted my arm. "Make the call and stop trying to protect me."

"Whoopee, I wanted to pick up some extra money. I just didn't

64

know it was going to be as an escort." I retrieved the crumpled paper from my jeans pocket.

When the guy on the phone asked how old I was, I lied. "Twenty-four."

He agreed to see me and gave me an address in a strip mall off Bee Ridge Road on the east side of Sarasota.

When we got there, I tried to back out.

Aunt Kay said, "Oh, stop being such a baby. What can possibly go wrong?"

Right then and there I should have pushed her out onto the pavement and driven away . . . fast.

CHAPTER 16

The escort agency was in a small brick building over a pizza store. The guy on the phone said to take the side entrance to the second floor, go down the hall past the modeling agency and photography studio to the end of the corridor and knock on the door of 204.

I tried to talk Aunt Kay into waiting in the truck but she kept insisting she was going with me.

At the door the stenciled name of the photo studio jogged my memory. "The last time I saw Holly was at Sarasota Mall last January. She was on the way to have pictures taken."

Aunt Kay's mouth turned down in a disapproving frown. "Photos cost her a small fortune over the years."

"She said something about a good omen."

"Holly was always talking some nonsense about omens and signs."

Inside the door Aunt Kay stopped dead and looked at the steep flight of stairs. "Oh," she said.

"I may want to get out of there in a hurry if things go wrong," I said. "It's better if you stay here. There's a bench in front of the pizza place."

She turned her sad and bewildered face to me. "But I don't want you to go alone."

I dug out my phone and opened it. "If I'm not back in twenty minutes you can call the cops, okay?"

She nodded, happier now that she was protecting me, but I wasn't at all certain she knew how to use a cell phone.

There was no name on the solid wood door. When no one answered my knock, I tried the door. It was locked.

A wave of relief washed over me. I was turning away and already planning my excuses to Aunt Kay when I heard the click of the catch. The door opened a crack. I could see it was still on a chain. I looked into the void of the open door and then I lowered my gaze.

The man I was looking down on read my surprise and gave me a look that I was guessing meant, "Eat shit and die, bitch." What he said was, "What do you want?"

"I'm Sherri. I just called you," I said in case he forgot.

"Yeah, I remember," he replied. "I also remember you said you were twenty-four."

"Yeah, well, I was once."

He closed the door and took off the chain and I stepped inside, into a room that reeked of pine air freshener.

I watched the guy walk back to his desk. He was about eight inches shorter than me, making him about four foot eleven in his snakeskin cowboy boots, but what he lacked in height he more than made up for in attitude.

"My name is Cal Vachess and I run the Angel Escort Agency." He was ruggedly handsome but his hands and his head looked oversized for his height. My mind, always ready to take a roll in the muck, wondered what other parts of him were normal size.

Something in my face must have betrayed my thoughts, perhaps I smiled, or perhaps he was just real good at knowing what people were thinking, but the look he gave me set my knees to wobbling. Then he flexed his shoulders, making his jacket bulge open to reveal a handgun in a leather shoulder holster.

Pity the jerk that treated Cal Vachess as a small amusement. My smirk was definitely gone even before he lifted the edge of his white linen jacket to show off the pistol a little better, just in case I'd missed it the first time. I was betting he let everyone know he was carrying so his size would no longer matter, a gun being a great equalizer. Everything about this guy said he was ready to back up the talk with the walk.

I looked away.

Circus prints covered the walls behind the oak desk. Southwest Florida was the winter home for the circus and the Ringlings built their estate on Sarasota Bay, making Sarasota a big circus town. You can find memorabilia all over the place.

The wall next to me was hung with black-and-white autographed photos of circus stars, from the high-wire to animal acts. I figured the tiny clowns, peeking out of a miniature fire truck, were more family history than souvenirs.

"So you're looking for a job," he said.

The desk held a notebook computer and two cell phones. That was it. No copier. No printer. It was a stripped-down paperless office, one that could be run out of a vehicle or shut down in a heartbeat.

I shook my head. "I want to ask you about a girl who worked for you."

"I'm not in the business of doing favors."

"I'll pay for information."

He jerked a thumb at a wooden chair. "Tell me what you want to know and I'll tell you how much it's going to cost you."

He sat in a high-back leather chair that made him look like a kid playing Daddy. He grabbed the edge of the desk and pulled himself up to it. "So, who are you interested in?"

"Her name was Holly Mitchell. She died Saturday night."

"The cops have already been here." He pointed to the door. "I got nothing for you so take off." He picked up a cell, flicked it open and thumbed the screen.

"The police think it was suicide. Why did they come here?"

"Ask them."

"I thought you were in the business of selling information."

"I don't have anything more for you. I have calls to make." His eyes went back to the screen.

"Holly was important to her family. I just need to know why she took her life. Her aunt needs to understand; she had to identify her as next of kin."

"Whatever happened to her had nothing to do with me. She hadn't even started working for me."

"You mean she worked somewhere else, a different agency?"

"No, I mean she had a full-time gig."

"Do you know who it was with . . . this full-time thing?"

"I'm not interested in past history. She was just one more bimbo. They come and they go. I don't have time to talk to them." He motioned to the door with the cell phone and said, "And I don't have time for you either." He was already accessing a number on his cell.

I stood up and took two steps towards the door. "Did Holly tell you she had a baby?"

His head jerked around to face me. "What?"

"A baby. Her name is Angel."

His eyes changed. "No shit?"

"Holly never told you?"

"Never."

"Strange, she told people everything. Not good at secrets, our Holly. She always confided in people, even the wrong ones."

His jaw hardened. "Well, she didn't confide in me. I hardly knew her, so if that's all you got, goodbye. I got work to do."

I was opening the door when he said, "Too bad you didn't come through that door ten years ago. I could have used you. You're too old now."

I looked over my shoulder at him and laughed.

An answering smile lit his face. "Tell you what, we still get a few old guys who aren't as particular." He flicked a card across his desk in my direction. "If you want to pick up a little cash give me a call."

"Do they bring their own nurses? I don't do potty duty."

And now he laughed. "See you around."

I sincerely hoped not but before I could feel relieved that it was over, the overpowering smell of expensive cologne filled my nose and a large man blocked the door.

His face was so much like Cal Vachess's they could have been twins, but this guy towered over me.

CHAPTER 17

"Hello there," he said with exaggerated warmth and slid forward until his face was way too close to mine.

I edged away but he moved closer, filling the void I'd created between us. My shoulder was up against the door jamb. I was trapped. Even if his nearness hadn't made me uncomfortable, his breath would have driven me back. I tilted my head away from the overwhelming scent of decay.

Perfectly tanned and looking like a male model, he was wearing a pink polo shirt, crisp khaki shorts and boat shoes with no socks. In his left ear was a diamond stud to match the diamond ring on his right hand, which he had planted on the door frame by my left ear.

"Hey, I know you, don't I?" he said.

I kept my face turned, my head tilted to the floor. "Nope."

"Sure I do."

Behind us Cal said, "She's just on her way out, Ryan." And then he added, "Goodbye."

"Ignore my brother." Ryan took my face in his hand and turned my head back to face him. I tried to turn away but his strong fingers held me fixed there. The intensity of Ryan's stare was unbearable, assessing me like he would a new purchase.

"If I don't know you, I'm certainly going to." He pressed his body up against mine.

"She's just leaving," Cal said.

Ryan ignored Cal and studied me, his forehead creasing, before he asked, "Really, come on now, aren't you someone I know?"

This guy was as high as a kite. Now call me a prude, but it was like the middle of a Monday morning. Even I knew Monday mornings are all about sobriety.

"Who do you know?" I asked.

"I know everyone," he said, exhaling a foul smell into my face. "Everyone." He wasn't high on alcohol.

"Then you're right. If you know everyone, you know me."

He grinned with delight. "I knew it."

"But I don't know you," I said.

He stuck his hand in between our shoulders for a shake. "Ryan Vachess. How can I . . ." He paused before adding, " . . . be of service?" And he meant the word *service*.

"Goodbye," Cal said loudly, shoving me out the door with his right hand as he pulled Ryan inside with his left.

Without ever looking at Cal, Ryan pushed him backwards, sending his brother crashing into the wall. Then Ryan reached out and recaptured my face in his hand, pulling me towards him by my jaw while moving my face from side to side, his eyes fixed on me, focused and intent.

I fought the urge to slap his hand away.

Cal recovered and said, "Get in here, Ryan. We have work to do."

"In a minute," Ryan said. His eyes never left my face. "Great bones. I can do wonderful things with them; get the lighting just right . . . haunting. I'm going to shoot in black and white. When do we start?"

"Did you take the pictures of Holly? You made her look real nice. Not like she normally looked at all."

He laughed. "No one comes to me to look normal, honey. I create the secret someone they always wanted to be . . . their inner fantasy. Holly Dolly was born to serve and submit, while you . . . well, you're something more interesting. You, I'll do in leather, the full treatment, whip, thigh-highs, all black and catlike. A predator." He growled at me.

"Ryan, shut up. She isn't here for that."

Ryan reached for my left hand. "No ring, so it isn't a bedroom shot for hubby. Are you coming to work for us?"

Cal's hand locked around his brother's forearm and he jerked Ryan into the office. Cal turned back to me and said, "Get out of here now."

I didn't move fast enough so he gave me a little push. I was barely out of the way when he slammed the door.

I went about ten feet down the hall before I stopped. I really wanted to know what they were talking about.

I tiptoed back to the varnished brown door and then leaned into it, straining to hear. Nothing.

There was the sound of a phone ringing but I couldn't make out another thing until there was a crash.

Cal's voice came through clearly now. "You stupid fuck. Get the hell out of here."

Before I could move, the door was jerked open. Cal stared at me. "What do you want now?"

The ice in his voice froze my brain. I couldn't think. I looked just beyond him to Ryan.

"It's me. She wants me." Ryan gave me a reptilian smile of joy and pointed a finger at me. "I told Cal you came looking for me."

Ryan started for the door but Cal held out his arm to stop him. "I said, 'What do want?'" Cal's outstretched arm held Ryan away from me.

"My keys?" My heart was pounding. "I forgot my keys."

Cal looked down at my hand and right at my keys.

"Oh," I said.

Cal said, "Was there anything else?"

"Stupid of me. Sorry."

Behind him Ryan slapped at Cal's hand and said, "Oh, she wants me . . ."

Before Ryan could finish Cal catapulted into action, slamming the door to 204.

I stared at the door in shock. I could hear them now, yelling and cursing at each other.

Their anger jolted me into action and I sprinted down the hall. I flew out the door.

Aunt Kay's eyes opened in surprise and she rose from the bench. I motioned to her. "Let's get the hell out of here."

A hard sun beat down and heat radiated back off the concrete—it had to be a hundred degrees. "Hurry," I said.

Aunt Kay couldn't wait until we were in the truck; she wanted to hear everything word for word and she wanted it right then.

"Don't talk." It was a day to move quickly from air conditioning to more air conditioning, but quick wasn't one of her dance steps. When we made it to the truck she demanded to know everything.

"I think Cal takes care of the escort service and Ryan looks after the modeling agency. He takes the sexy pictures that wives give to their husbands and does portfolios for models."

"And they get girls for their escort service that way?"

"Probably."

"I bet this Ryan convinced Holly that he could make her famous, that posing for nasty pictures was just a step on the road to success. Didn't Marilyn Monroe start out that way? She did those calendars. You remember. There was one where she was stretched out on red satin. She was famous for that picture. I can see how Holly would fall for Ryan's line."

Her breath was coming in pants.

I said, "This is too much for you. You should be home resting and getting your strength back."

She scowled at me. "You trying to slack off on me?"

"No, but I am a little worried you might die on me."

"You let me worry about that."

She fanned her face and took a few breaths before she went on. "That Ryan passed me as he was going in. He didn't look well to me."

"He spends too much time on a tanning bed and he's too thin, plus he was high as a kite. There's a lot of scary stuff being manufactured out there right now. Something chemical. Ice maybe, which would explain his bad breath and his thinness and why he was high at this time of the day."

She asked, "Why . . . why does it explain all that?"

"You don't eat on ice and don't drink enough, so bacteria builds up in your mouth. Gives you stinky breath and eventually rots your teeth."

We'd been lucky to find a bit of shade from the bank across from the pizza joint—the sun hadn't moved far enough around to rob us of that protection. "Isn't it strange that Holly named her baby Angel?" I said as I cranked up the air and slid the windows down.

Aunt Kay considered that question. "Maybe it's because we always think of babies as angels. First thing we say is, 'What a little angel.' Maybe Holly called her baby Angel and then found Angel Photography. You know Holly. She'd think it was a sign, finding Angel Photography."

She fastened her seat belt, slipping her right arm through it so the shoulder strap was behind her. "Do you think they know where Angel is?"

I had no answer.

Just as I was about to hit the streets I slammed on the brakes and put the gearshift into reverse. "Let's see if we can find their rides."

"Why?"

I shot backwards into the slot we'd just left. "Just in case we see them again." Somewhere in my brain I'd already processed the fact that I'd made a huge error. While I never wanted to see either of the Vachess brothers again, I didn't think it was likely to happen.

It was a fair-sized lot and I cruised slowly through it, considering all the cars until I came to a red Mustang. I pointed out the window. "That's Ryan's." The license read HOT PIC.

Aunt Kay craned her neck. "Which one is Cal's?"

"It must be modified so he can drive it," I said.

"Then get out and check in the cars." She was already undoing her belt.

"Forget it." I headed for the exit. "Getting caught listening at the door was bad enough. If they find me inspecting their cars . . ." I didn't want to think about that outcome. "We're done here."

She tried to swivel around and look out the back window. "Let's wait here and see if Ryan comes out."

"Not on your life. He already thinks I came hunting him. Meth heads are paranoid and dangerous and there's a new type of meth on the street that makes people truly crazy. There's no predicting what he'll do if he finds us here. Cal was clear he didn't want his brother anywhere near me."

She frowned. "Why?"

"I don't know but I'm pretty sure he has a very good reason. No telling what's going on with that Ryan. He's one sick scumbag. I'm done with him."

If only it had been true.

CHAPTER 18

After we'd put a block between us and the Vachess brothers, I said, "Now what?"

Aunt Kay started digging in her bag. She came out with an envelope, squinted at it, and then handed it to me. "This is the address where Holly lived before she moved to the Jade Towers."

I glanced at it and handed it back. "Newtown, a different world from where she ended up, that's for sure." I hit US 301 and headed north. "She's been gone from this address for ages. We're not likely to find anything."

She gave me a look. I was guessing it said, "Since I'm paying for your time, and paying well, shut up and drive." Apparently chauffeurs aren't allowed to have opinions.

In Sarasota, well, in all Florida, the price of real estate is dependent upon how close to the water you are. Holly's old apartment on Adler Street was far from the water and from the Jade Towers in price and safety. In the northeast corner of Sarasota, almost to Bradenton, the Newtown area hadn't gone upscale yet as had everything else with a Sarasota address.

In this part of town there was still a bar on every corner, adult video stores and strip clubs. By day, it was acceptable. After dark it was what it had always been, a place to move quickly, preferably at a run, to avoid encounters with fellow members of the human race.

I parked right in front of the address and studied the horseshoe-shaped complex. An abandoned couch, lying on its back with the cushions falling off, clogged the narrow courtyard. Trash piled up against the buildings and was tangled in the dying bushes flanking the steps to the central hall of each unit. With buckling concrete and broken windows, the whole thing was all just passing time until the next urban renewal project.

I had a good look around for danger. An old man sat nodding on a broken-down kitchen chair in the shade of the building across the street, but other than that nothing moved in the heat.

"Why don't you wait here until I see if there's anyone who remembers Holly."

A high-riding car cruised by, taking a good look at us. Even though all the windows were up, the music of rap throbbed from the muscle machine. The old man across the street didn't even lift his chin off his chest.

Aunt Kay fanned her face gently with her little Chinese fan and looked out the window.

I said, "There won't be an elevator, just three flights of stairs."

She sighed. "All right, but don't give up too easily." She opened her purse and took out a photograph. "It's the last one I have of Holly."

In this picture Holly was in her brunette days. It hardly looked like the Holly I remembered, but then maybe this was the real Holly and the one I thought I knew was the false one. Certainly the Holly working for an escort service wasn't the Holly I'd met. I turned the print over and read the name of the photographer on the back.

Watching me, Aunt Kay said. "I already called them while I was waiting for you to show up. They took that picture three years ago and no one remembers Holly."

"I'll leave the motor running so you'll have air."

"I've lived in Florida all my life; a little heat isn't going to bother me." Her window slid down. "No sense in polluting the air and wasting gas."

"These conditions are dangerous."

Aunt Kay looked like just about anything could kill her.

"We're going to break another record today."

"I'll be all right." She pulled her cropped slacks up over her swollen knees and sat there with her hands planted on her thighs, Buddha-like and immovable.

I lowered my window for her. "There's more water in the back if you need it."

There was no security system in the building and no super either. There wasn't even central air in this crumbling structure, so all the apartments had air conditioners hanging from their windows at the front of the building.

The front door was wedged open to catch any breeze, but even so the hall was stifling and breathless, filled with the odor of stale cooking and garbage. I was boiling in my own sweat by the time I reached the third floor and knocked at Holly's former apartment. No one answered. I knocked at the neighbor's across the hall. Nothing.

Now this was annoying.

I knocked at the other two doors on the third floor. If anyone was home they weren't interested in a visitor.

I went down to the second floor and started there, working my way down the hall and coming up with two annoyed people who didn't know Holly and weren't interested in knowing me either.

On the first floor, the sounds of a couple arguing had me tapping lightly on the door. The door swung violently open and a man, barefoot and wearing only boxers, glared at me. "What?"

I showed him the picture of Holly and asked, "Do you remember this woman? She lived in apartment 302."

"No," he said. The door slammed shut.

No one else was home on that floor and I arrived back at the street dripping with perspiration and totally pissed off. Aunt Kay was going to insist I come back at night, when people were home from work, and do it all over again. That was not my idea of a fun evening. More than that, this was no neighborhood to be in after dark.

An aged Honda, the trunk covered in Jesus fish, pulled in beside the sidewalk and died. A pretty young woman wearing a white halter dress got out of the car. She smiled over the roof of the Honda at me. Her smile showed impossibly gleaming white teeth.

At last, someone genuinely glad to see me. I gave a little wave and said, "Hi."

"Back at you." She opened the back door and dragged out a huge shiny vinyl bag covered in buckles. When she slammed the door shut she was already moving.

I intercepted her. "I'm looking for Holly Mitchell." I pointed to the middle building. "She lives in 302; well, she did a bit ago. Do you know her?" I waved the photograph in front of her.

She slung the bag over her left shoulder and frowned at the picture. "No, but then I just moved in and it isn't exactly the kind of place where you know your neighbors." She walked around me and hit the sidewalk moving fast.

"Wait," I called to the already retreating bare shoulders.

She swung to face me, walking backwards away from me in her high-heeled sandals.

I followed her. "Is there anyone in the building who might know about Holly?"

She hesitated and frowned. "Yeah, the witch who lives on the main floor, she thinks she owns the building. Sunny her name is, a bartender at the Flamingo two blocks over." She pointed to her left. "It's a horrible place, but then so is Sunny." She was moving again.

"Would she be there now?"

She considered it and said. "I don't know. I don't have anything to do with Sunny. Bartenders aren't the kind of people you want to know, are they?" She gave a jaunty little wave and spun on her toes before jogging for the front door.

That girl knew how to survive in neighborhoods like this.

CHAPTER 19

With flyers and dead leaves piled up in the small alcove at the door, the Flamingo bar looked abandoned. There was a big sign on the glass that said the Flamingo would be going out of business come Saturday. FOR SALE signs already covered the building but there weren't going to be any takers. The only thing that was going to happen to this property was a bulldozer and another high-rise and, given the economy, that would be years away.

Another sign said that the Flamingo offered happy hour from eleven in the morning until closing time. You can't get happier than that.

At the door of the Flamingo a drink-ruined and urine-soaked man held out his hand to Aunt Kay. "Can you spare some change?"

I stepped in between him and Aunt Kay. "No." The volume of my voice left him in no doubt about of my feelings.

We stepped into a dark interior that smelled of unwashed bodies, stale beer and every tub of grease that had been eaten in the place. The three drinkers, strung out along the bar, looked up as the door opened and then went back to staring into their glasses. The flickering fluorescent went unnoticed, the buzzing noise just one more small annoyance in lives made up of a long list of such things.

The décor was put together from garage sales on the wrong side of town and featured lots of dark faux wood and plastic. The whole place should have been taken back to the dumpster it came from, though I sort of coveted the flashing pink flamingo over the bar.

The bartender matched the decoration, worn out, cheap and plastic. Her straw-blonde hair was a reminder of a fright wig from Halloween and her deep smoker's bark almost drowned out the hurt-dog-wailing that was passing for music. She leaned on the bar with both tattooed arms locked in front of her. This unfortunate pose exposed the parts of her speckled breasts that her one-size-too-small top wasn't already showing off. A smiling sun was tattooed on her left breast. It didn't improve the picture.

For a brief moment, I wondered if I was looking at my future. I fought down that gruesome thought, not sure if I wanted to live with the answer. There was one ray of sunlight. At least no one could see my tattoo, not even me.

Aunt Kay didn't know about bars, didn't know you should wait for a second at the door to feel out trouble before you make your move. Unaware that you need to get the vibe of the place and carefully pick out who you choose to drink beside, she rumbled right over to the bar and planted herself in front of the tender.

The bartender looked at Aunt Kay as though she might be peddling bibles. "Whadda you want?" Tips probably weren't a big part of her income.

Aunt Kay set her big old purse on the bar. "Are you Sunny?"

The tender looked to me and then back to Aunt Kay before she gave a quick nod.

"Well, I just want a word, dear."

Before Sunny could say she wasn't a visitor's guide, I added, "We'll have two sodas." Sunny gave me a searing look. For a heartbeat I thought she was going to point us in the direction of the door, but instead she shoved two glasses into a pan of ice and shot some soda at them. She frowned as she dropped the glass in front of me. There was something about me that turned her right off, but then, I have that affect on a lot of people.

Aunt Kay gave the bartender one of those sweet smiles that made you want to sit down for warm cookies and cold milk. She picked up the glass Sunny thumped down on the bar with a grateful "Thank you," like she'd been handed a treasure.

I edged the glass towards me and stared down at the brownish liquid.

"Oh, this is just what I need." Aunt Kay held the sweating glass of soda up to her cheek. "It's so hot out there."

Hadn't Aunt Kay noticed that it was barely cooler in here? Maybe she was making nice, something I've yet to learn. Whatever it was, Aunt Kay was going to get a lot further with Sunny than I ever could.

"I hope you can help me with a little problem," Aunt Kay said.

Sunny's mouth twitched, chewing on the words to drive us out the door, but there's something about Aunt Kay that makes people behave better than they normally would.

Aunt Kay set down her soda. "You see, dear, my niece, a sweet girl, died last night."

Aunt Kay had Sunny's attention now. She pulled Holly's picture out of her purse and slid it across the bar. "I want to know why Holly died and I want to know what happened to her little girl."

Sunny looked down at the picture. She might be tough but it hit her. Emotion rippled across her face and she sucked her lips in between her teeth. Sunny hadn't known Holly was dead.

"How?" Sunny asked.

Like all great storytellers, Aunt Kay took her time now that she had her audience's attention. Using the bar, she pulled herself up onto a wooden stool and settled her behind on the seat that was undersized for her.

Sunny was experienced in listening to thousands of stories, most of which she didn't want to hear. She waited, without asking any questions and not showing all that much interest now she had herself under control.

"That's better," Aunt Kay said, as she propped her short legs up on the top rung of the stool and got comfortable. She drank deeply from her glass.

Sunny blinked. "How did Holly die?"

"Suicide."

Sunny jerked back as if she'd been hit. "Oh, shit."

"That's why I need your help."

"Holly wouldn't kill herself." Sunny's angry and outraged reply was loud enough to have the drinkers down the bar looking up and taking some interest before they went back to their glasses.

Sunny looked to me as if I might want to explain things.

I shrugged and Sunny turned back to Aunt Kay, who said, "I need to understand what happened to her. I know so little about this last little bit of her life. I'm finding it hard to accept her death."

Sunny looked at me again. "Holly wouldn't kill herself." It was as if she was challenging me.

"She left a note," I said. "The police are pretty sure it was suicide but they'll do an autopsy."

Aunt Kay cut in. "I had to identify her body. So distressing." Her shoulders rounded and she seemed to shrink into herself. I wanted to hug her.

Sunny picked up Aunt Kay's half-empty glass, added ice and more soda and set it gently back in front of her. This time she even brought a little paper napkin to put the glass on.

Aunt Kay smiled. "Thank you, dear. Can you tell me anything about Holly? Do you know where her baby is?"

Sunny shook her head. "I haven't seen Holly in months. People move on; you know how it is."

"Yes, but I know Holly." Aunt Kay took a sip of her soda. "She was the kind of girl who kept in touch. Sometimes her idle chatter could be annoying, making you wish she'd forget she knew you."

The corner of Sunny's mouth twitched, not quite a smile.

"I'm sure she called you," Aunt Kay said softly.

I wondered why Aunt Kay was so sure of this but Sunny gave an embarrassed shrug. "Well, yeah, she'd call in the middle of some program I was trying to watch and talk about the new nail polish she'd just bought or some person she'd met, tell me the whole life story of someone I didn't know. She was a hard person to discourage."

She looked around. "Maybe I didn't try too hard. She was always so damn cheerful and a lot more interesting than the people that I normally listen to."

Aunt Kay laughed. "That's my Holly all right." But just as quickly her smile disappeared. "If that was true, why would she kill herself? What had changed? Was she depressed?"

"Like I said, I haven't talked to her in months. Before that, she'd breeze in here and chat away like a bloody bird. Didn't matter who was here, she'd chat to them all." Sunny almost smiled. "It was like someone blew out a wall and let the fresh air in."

She glanced down the bar at the three men and then took a deep breath. "I can't tell you a lot, but what do you want to know?"

"Did you know Angel?"

"Yeah," and now Sunny's face relaxed into her first real smile, the one that revealed where she got her name. "She was beautiful. Delicate, you know, with perfect little rosebud lips. Her face never looked, well . . . it was like a perfect little doll's. She was . . ." her voice faltered and stopped. Someone called her name from the end of the bar. Relief flooded her face. "I have to take care of these guys," she said and left.

"Do you think she can help us?" Aunt Kay whispered.

"Maybe." I didn't add, "If she wants to." My guess was that Sunny was not into helping anyone. That gets burned out of you pretty fast behind a bar, and you start to play dumb and stay neutral. I've got a friend who calls it "being Switzerland," not getting involved. It's the only way to survive.

When Sunny came down the bar to join us again, sympathy and sentimentality had been flushed down the sink with the last of the booze in the dirty glasses. "All I can tell you is Angel was born just after Christmas. Couple of months later Holly was gone. She stopped coming around."

Aunt Kay smiled. "It's a busy time with a new baby. So much to do. Of course she wouldn't bring a baby in here, would she? No offense, but it isn't the sort of place babies would be welcome."

Sunny picked up my untouched glass and set it in a plastic pan with the other dirty glasses.

"Do you have a car?" Aunt Kay asked.

Sunny's yes was reluctant.

"Did Holly?"

"On what she made? No."

"She was working as a beautician, right?"

"Yeah, right up until the week before Angel was born. I told her all the fumes, nail polish and stuff, wasn't good for the baby but she didn't listen."

Aunt Kay's voice was soft and gentle. "I don't suppose she had a choice, did she?"

Sunny frowned. "No, no choice. That's the problem with being poor, no choices."

"And she would have had so many appointments before and after having the baby. It's so difficult with public transit and taxis are expensive—it would be so nice to be picked up and dropped off."

Sunny scowled.

"You drove her places, didn't you?"

Poor Sunny, she so didn't want to be caught in the role of Good Samaritan. "Yeah, sometimes."

"Every woman needs someone there for them when they have a baby. It's just too hard to do alone." Aunt Kay reached out and patted Sunny's hand. "Thank you for taking care of Holly."

Sunny took her time pulling her hand away.

"She was a good kid," Sunny said. "Just not too bright, you know?" Again the frown. "No, that's not right. She was bright enough. She just didn't have common sense, just didn't know what end was up if you know what I mean. And she didn't seem to learn from her mistakes."

"Few of us do," Aunt Kay said. "Did you ever meet the father?"

"She didn't introduce me but I saw him coming and going, wore a uniform."

"What kind of a uniform?"

"A cop, he was a cop."

"Ah, yes," Aunt Kay said with a nod. "Was there only the one man in Holly's life?"

"She wasn't that kind of girl," Sunny was angry again. "She loved him, said she had since they were kids, but the bastard took off as soon as he knocked her up. Never saw him again after Holly started to show. I tell you, I ever see that guy again, cop or no, I see him on the street, I'm going to run him down."

"If it's any conciliation, he didn't know about the baby. That's not why he stopped seeing her." Aunt Kay finished her drink and set it down on the sodden and tattered napkin. "The problem is no one seems to know where the baby is now. For my own peace of mind I have to know where Angel is, know that she's safe."

Sunny frowned and crossed her arms over her chest. "I don't know anything more about Angel."

Sunny wasn't going to win any prizes for lying.

"How long did Holly stay in your apartment building after Angel was born?" I asked.

Sunny gave it some thought. "Holly and I spent Christmas Day together. It was only a couple of weeks before Angel was born. I nuked two frozen turkey dinners and we watched those stupid Christmas shows on TV. No more than six weeks. Her money ran out. She couldn't work and look after the baby. She told me she was going to move in with family."

Beside me Aunt Kay made a funny strangling sound. I reached out and put an arm around her shoulders and asked, "Did Holly mention any names?"

"Naw, just said she would be in touch. She called once." Sunny hesitated. "She sounded a bit strange, like she was pretending she was fine but she wasn't. I didn't push for details. Guess I should have." She sighed and then admitted, "I didn't want to know."

"That is true of all of us," I told her. "We all have our own lives and don't want to worry about anyone else's."

Sunny nodded and turned away, heading for the other end of the bar although no one down there was ordering drinks.

"I don't think we're going to get anything more from Sunny," Aunt Kay said.

I watched Sunny without replying.

Aunt Kay said, "I think we might as well go."

"We'll stay a little longer."

When Sunny came back she pointed at me and said, "Holly had a picture of you and her on the beach."

"I don't remember it."

"She showed me an article about you . . . about that woman who attacked you." She was waiting for me to add something. Damned if I knew what.

Finally she said, "She said you two were real close, told anyone who would listen about you."

"She was exaggerating."

"She told me that you owned a fancy restaurant and that she'd worked there helping you run it."

I snorted. "Holly couldn't run a vacuum."

Sunny grinned. "I didn't say I believed her. I thought Holly might have gone to live with you or that you might have taken Angel."

"Not me."

She nodded.

I said, "So where's Angel?"

Sunny considered the question. When she'd made up her mind she said, "Okay. Before Angel was born, I gave Holly the name of a lawyer I know. He arranges private adoptions. Holly didn't want it. She figured Daddy couldn't live without her and would come running back to play happy family. Wasn't gonna happen, but you couldn't tell Holly. She was always so naive and certain there was a happy ending just around the corner. She was going to be discovered by a big modeling agency or some big producer, never mind that she was already too old, she still thought it would happen, always having photos taken. Do you know how much those guys charge?" Anger, quick and volcanic, overflowed. "Ripping her off and taking advantage of her."

Sunny slapped a gray dishrag onto the counter and mopped at the damp rings left by my glass. "When Holly called me, about . . ." Sunny thought about it a minute, "must have been sometime around Easter, well, by then the fizz had gone out of her. She was just like the rest of us then. Don't know what destroyed it. Didn't ask. I did ask about Angel."

She reached beneath the bar and brought out a pack of smokes. With the bar about to close she was no longer worried about bylaws or health authorities who had never breached the front door. She lit her cigarette and drew deeply before saying, "Holly said she'd given Angel to friends." She was glaring at me as though she held me personally responsible. "Holly said it was temporary, said she was going to get Angel back in a few months. I don't know if she believed it. I didn't."

Sunny's permanent scowl was replaced by a flash of pain. "I just know Holly no longer had her baby. I hope she found a good home for Angel."

"We want to make sure," I said. "Do you remember anything else?"

Sunny shook her head. "That's all I know."

"I'm going to need the name of the lawyer."

Sunny frowned.

"Don't worry; no one will ever know where we got the name," I said. "If they insist on knowing, I'll say Holly told me."

Sunny stared at the entrance where the old man stood with his hands shielding his eyes and his face pressed up against the glass.

It took Sunny some time to decide. "You see that guy at the door?" She gave a nod in his direction.

"Yes."

"He used to drive a school bus until he killed a kid. Seems the kid dropped something and stopped to pick it up. The driver saw the rest of the kids had crossed the road and drove off. He killed the boy kneeling in front of the bus picking up the things that spilled out of his backpack. That guy's a no-account drunk now but Holly was kind to him. Holly gave him money. She was a good person. She . . ." Her face did a funny shift and she looked away for a moment and swiped at her nose.

When she faced us she was strong and defiant again. "Well, in a few days . . . when the Flamingo closes Saturday night, a lot of people will have to find a new place to be miserable, including me and that guy."

Sunny reached beneath the bar and brought out an order pad. She wrote on it and then pulled off the sheet and pushed it towards me.

I put my hand on the paper. "Do you have a job . . . somewhere to go?"

"Yup, I'm going to swallow my pride and go back to a place I never should have left."

"Good luck to you." I picked up the paper and replaced it with a bill. Sunny looked at it and sucked in some more smoke. She didn't offer change and I didn't ask for any.

Aunt Kay stopped outside the door and pulled some bills out of her wallet. Handing them to the panhandler, she said, "This is from Holly."

CHAPTER 20

Even though I was wearing sunglasses, the pounding sun made me squint. We walked slowly towards my red pickup with Aunt Kay leaning heavily on my arm as if she were about to drop dead from the skyrocketing temperature and exertion.

"Let's have a bite and then I'll take you home."

"I'd like something to eat, but we aren't quitting yet. I'm paying for your time, remember?"

"When you keep mentioning it, how can I forget?"

Aunt Kay said, "Let's go see that lawyer."

"I'm not going anywhere until I eat."

Aunt Kay gave a huge sigh. "You never change."

"You either, thank goodness."

We went through our routine to get her in the truck and I promised myself I would watch for a hardware store where I could buy a small step.

I stopped for a traffic light, still feeling for cooler air. "Please don't stop," I told the vent. Life without air would be unbearable.

I held my hand over the vent, trying to decide if the thin trickle of air blowing out was any cooler than what was already in the cab and thinking about what Sunny had told us. "Why would Holly talk about me?"

Aunt Kay fanned her face and looked out the window. "You know Holly—she talked about everyone she knew."

I saw golden arches in the distance and changed lanes. When I started to turn in Aunt Kay said, "Not on your life. If we're eating out, I want somewhere nice."

I started to protest but she stopped me with, "I'll buy."

"You just said my favorite words. Where would you like to go?"

"Rosa's. I haven't been there in years. We used to come up once a month for a Saturday night dinner. It would be nice to go there again."

Three blocks later I pulled into Rosa's, the best Italian restaurant in Sarasota.

But any enjoyment of Rosa's disappeared as the door to the restaurant opened and a couple emerged. They were laughing as they turned and walked away from us.

Bernice had put on weight. She'd always been skeletal but now, as she led the way across the parking lot of the restaurant, her ass was doing a rumba. I don't think she used to have an ass, never mind one that could dance.

And the hand that reached out to pat that dancing round mound of my ex-mother-in-law belonged to my old man, Tully Jenkins.

"Why are we stopping here? Why aren't you parking?" Aunt Kay said.

"We aren't eating just yet."

"What is it, what's wrong?"

"That's what I want to know."

I watched them get into her BMW and back out, leaving my dad's beat-up old pickup sitting there, and then I followed Bernice out of the parking lot. They didn't go far, just to the Palms Motel. They parked, got out of the car, still laughing like teenagers and holding hands as they went up the outside stairs to a room on the second floor. The door closing behind them was like a kick in the gut.

Aunt Kay pointed at the door. "That's your father, isn't it?"

"Yeah, that's him all right."

"And the woman, do you know her?"

"Oh, yeah, too well."

I'd married Jimmy Travis before I was twenty and in the end the whole sorry experience was a good reason to weep. Don't get me wrong, it started out great but my bliss was short-lived. My idea of marriage didn't include the groom having sex with a friend of the family after the rehearsal dinner.

And Jimmy hadn't been the only source of my tears. Bernice Travis, my former mother-in-law, had done her bit. Our hate for each other was deep and everlasting, growing like a cancer throughout my life with Jimmy. And even after Jimmy's death our wars went on. Now my old man was feeling her up in public.

Aunt Kay said, "Oh," with shock and surprise in her voice. "I remember her from your wedding; I know who she is."

"The bitch is just doing this to get back at me."

"Maybe this has nothing to do with you."

"You mean I'm having delusions? They didn't just walk up those stairs and into a motel room?"

"Whatever you believe about her, however much she may wish to hurt you, why is your father with her? He doesn't want to upset you, does he?"

"My dad never needs any reason to sleep with a woman beyond availability."

I opened the door of the truck.

Aunt Kay grabbed my arm, holding me back. "Where are you going?"

I jerked my arm away. "I'm going to say hello to my father."

Aunt Kay threw her hands in the air with frustration, or maybe disgust, as I slammed the door.

CHAPTER 21

Bernice opened the door to the motel room but I looked past her to Tully. He was naked to the waist and barefoot.

I looked up from the gray hairs on his chest and I asked, "Why Bernice, why choose her? There are lots of nice ladies about."

"Oh, honey, whatever would I want with a nice lady?" He laughed a deep belly laugh and came to stand beside Bernice, putting his right arm around her and pulling her close to his side. "We'll all be in a grave soon enough; there's no use being bored to death first, and one thing about Bernice, she ain't never boring."

I had to agree with him there. She was so interesting, I'd spent many an hour dreaming of her lying in a casket while I smiled down at her.

But my dad wasn't done with his own joke. He patted Bernice's rump and said, "She's like that old pickup of Jimmy's that you like so well—seen a lot of use but she's got a few miles left in her yet." He laughed again. "Now was there something you wanted, sugar?"

Aunt Kay didn't offer any sympathy, quite the opposite. "You have no one to blame but yourself. What they do isn't any of your business."

"You don't know what I've been through with that woman."

"I remember. You and Bernice Travis were like two scorpions dropped in a paper bag, ready to fight to the death and not once thinking of joining forces to break through the sack."

"I'm not in the mood for philosophy."

"Well, here's a little more. If you don't change your ways, it won't be over until one of you is dead."

"As long as it's Bernice, it works for me."

"That's a long useless time to hate."

I jammed the gearshift into drive. "Bernice is doing this to get at me."

"Everything isn't about you."

My childhood view of Aunt Kay was undergoing a rapid change. Where was the kind, understanding woman who was always on my side? "You don't understand."

Aunt Kay laughed. "The thing is I understand too well. You and Bernice both loved Jimmy and you couldn't bear sharing."

My anger shifted from Bernice to Aunt Kay. "I'll take you home."

"But we have to see the lawyer."

"We'll do it tomorrow."

"Look here, I'm paying you to do a job."

"So fire me. We're going home."

By the time I'd gone five blocks I'd broken multiple laws and nearly run over an old couple. Washed by waves of violence, I dredged up every mean word and action Bernice had used against me until every injustice was new and fresh. No way I wanted anything more to do with Bernice. She had a way of cutting your pride to ribbons and turning your soul to dust, so if she was in Tully's life, he was out of mine.

It was a long, silent trip back to Jacaranda.

When we pulled into the driveway, Aunt Kay said, "Feel better?"

"Not if you're going to fire me."

She sighed. "Just don't try this again."

I headed for the Sunset. At the intersection where I make the left turn to the beach stood the church of perpetual neediness, with a permanent thermometer of donations standing higher than its cross.

I'm not sure why that sign was so infuriating. Maybe it's because I was always irritated those days. I was glaring at the sign and telling myself to take a deep breath when the door of the church rectory opened and out stepped Zach Maguire, Holly's former boyfriend. What was he doing coming out of church in the middle of the day?

I thought I'd make sure he knew about Holly and see if he could tell me anything about her I didn't already know. More than that, now that my anger had cooled, I was terrified that Aunt Kay might drop me and I'd lose my chance to save the Sunset. How could I have risked that? Instead of turning left for the Sunset I followed Zach back to the bank on Main Street, pulling into an empty spot beside him.

The Mexican restaurant next to the bank was sending out heavenly smells, reminding me I'd missed lunch. My stomach growled.

"Hi Zach."

He lifted his head to look at me. A sad, beaten puppy, he barely knew I was there. "Oh, hi Sherri."

"I guess you heard about Holly?"

It was like I'd struck him. I thought he was going to break into tears.

"I'm sorry," I said. "I know you were close to Holly."

He nodded. "Her mother came in today and told me."

"Had you seen Holly lately?"

He shook his head no and then changed his mind and nodded. "I haven't seen her in over a year. She called me though." He turned away.

"Why did Holly call you?"

His eyes flicked to the bank. I hustled around him and blocked his path.

"I should get back to work. I told them I'd just be gone an hour."

"You went to church, to confession?"

He looked at me in alarm. "What's it to you?"

"Well, I just thought when someone dies sometimes we feel guilty."

Zach looked down at the keys still in his hand. "I did something awful."

I sucked in my breath but Zach wasn't paying any attention to me.

"Holly said she needed help, needed money. I told her I couldn't help her and then she killed herself."

I let out the breath I'd been holding. "Don't beat yourself up. Holly had no right to expect anything from you. She dropped you pretty quick when it suited her."

"I wanted to marry her."

Even I couldn't ask about the baby now. "Did she tell you why she wanted money?"

He shook his head. "I haven't seen her since she moved up to Sarasota."

"Did she tell you anything else?"

Again he shook his head. "She just told me she was in trouble and needed money."

"Did she mention Angel?"

Zach's head came up and his face flushed. "Who's Angel?"

"Oh, just someone she knew. Someone she loved. Maybe Angel helped her."

"I hope so," he said. "I hope I wasn't her last chance."

I went back to the truck and called Aunt Kay to tell her about Zach and to make peace. "I'm pretty sure he doesn't know anything about Angel."

"He still might know Holly had a baby and where she is even if he doesn't know her name."

"Damn."

"You might want to chat with him again."

"Why don't you give me a check to put in the bank and then I'll have an excuse to go back and talk to him?"

She laughed. "Nice try."

She was silent for a bit. "We should have gone to the lawyer."

"If we had, I wouldn't have talked to Zach."

"Maybe we can still see the lawyer. Why don't you call and see if he'll see us tonight."

"I'm a little busy."

"And I'm a little old with not a lot of time to wait."

"Some sweet little old lady you turned out to be."

"Sorry to shatter your illusions."

"And there were so few left. We'll have a full day tomorrow, promise. I think you should rest."

Her noise of complete disgust wiped out all thoughts I had about Aunt Kay being a lady. "Let me worry about my health, about the weather, about everything that distracts you, and just pay attention to what needs doing. I expect a lot more than I'm getting for my money."

Yet one more disappointed customer in my life.

CHAPTER 22

At the Sunset I stood at the window and watched the bright green birds that never seemed to settle. They moved from branch to branch, flying up with harsh complaint and then settling down again.

I turned away. I still had to deal with losing Isaak. A restaurant can run without birds for entertainment but not without a chef.

I went into my office and called Miguel in from the kitchen.

Miguel was almost as devoted to the Sunset as I was. We'd both worked at the Sunset when Miss Emma had owned it and now we worked side by side, through long grueling hours, to do whatever it took to keep the Sunset alive.

Miguel had started working in a kitchen at fourteen, so although he had no formal training he had lots of experience. When he came into the office he was dressed in a white chef's coat and the black-and-white houndstooth-checked pants of a chef. Looking like a professional upped my confidence in him.

With skin like polished leather, an eagle beak of a nose and straight black hair, Miguel had the profile of a face carved on an Aztec ruin, but behind his severe exterior was an exuberant and joyous being.

I told him about Isaak leaving. He just nodded and waited for what came next. Miguel wasn't surprised at the news.

"You knew?" I was hurt that he hadn't warned me.

He shrugged. "He is a restless kind of guy."

That was all I was going to get out of him, so I let it drop. "So, will you take over?"

His face lit up and his white teeth flashed. "I've been watching. I know everything Isaak makes, can do everything he does." He rubbed his palms together. "I even know the new recipes he's been trying out. Those fancy dishes he'll be serving up north?" He jabbed a finger at the floor. "We'll be having them right here."

"You memorized all his recipes by watching him?"

He waggled his hand back and forth and then pulled something out of his breast pocket. "Every recipe he ever prepared is right here on this cute little memory stick."

"That's probably illegal."

"Then you likely don't want to know about it." He grinned and put his forefinger to his lips. "You wouldn't look good in orange and I'm too pretty to go to jail so let's say no more about it."

He slipped the memory stick back into the pocket of his jacket, grinning like a fool. "Nobody needs to know."

I raised my hand as if I were swearing an oath. "One more guilty secret I'll take to my grave."

But Miguel wasn't interested in our shared culpability. "I know I'm not trained like Isaak but I've watched every step. I can create every single one of his recipes. He's been practicing all kinds of new ones for the new restaurant."

"Serves him right then." Seems my morals are just like my workout clothes, nice and elastic. "If he's been creating menus for someone else while he was working for me, he deserves to have his recipes stolen. I probably have some right to them if they were created on my time." I was beginning to like this more and more. Truth was, if I was breaking some law by using Isaak's recipes, it would be the smallest law I'd ever violated.

"I know you can do it, Miguel."

I stood up and went towards Miguel with my hand outstretched. "You and I have put in too much hard work to lose the Sunset now. You'll do great."

He took my hand. "Especially with that lovely big raise you're going to give me."

"What?" I tried to pull my hand back but Miguel held on. "I can't afford to give you a raise."

He smiled. "Can you afford not to give me a raise?" He was right to be so sure of himself. I needed him.

"That's blackmail."

"Yes, oh, yes, exactly." He gave my hand a vigorous shake. "I learned from a master." He gave a slight bow.

I thought things were looking up, but I was disabused of that idea when Cal Vachess walked into the bar. But why not? My life was a circus so he fit right in.

I gave my bad imitation of Humphrey Bogart. "Of all the gin joints in all the world, why'd you have to walk into this one?"

Cal grinned and answered, "I decided I'd been a little too hasty. Maybe some guys wouldn't find you a total skank."

"If you're waiting to be thanked for that compliment you can forget it. Where's the brother?"

"Why do all the girls want Ryan?"

"God, I have no idea."

The sincerity of my reply made him laugh. Then he grew serious and said, "Nature makes mistakes."

"Oh, I don't know," I said, polishing the bar in front of him. "Sometimes she gets it right. You're dangerous enough just as you are and Ryan is just plain scary."

He laughed again but his amusement disappeared when he looked at the barstools, which were nearly as tall as him. Frustration and then raw anger infused his face.

Five-foot-tall women have trouble climbing up on those damn things and they can do it much more gracefully than any man. The stools were the one thing I'd done wrong when I'd rebuilt the Sunset after Hurricane Myrna and the first thing I was going to change when someone dropped a load of cash in my lap.

"Are you in a hurry for a drink or can I go check on things out front first?"

"No, go ahead," he said graciously. "For you, I'll wait."

No worries about him raiding the cash register, he'd need a pogo stick to get near it. So while he saved his dignity and got settled, I went out to talk to Gwen.

The Sunset was as busy as if it were a holiday weekend in high season. It seemed like all Jacaranda needed a little cheering up, even if it was only a palm tree full of parrots, and they'd decided to blow the budget and come out for dinner. Everyone knew this was only a temporary perch for our exotic birds and by tomorrow they'd be gone, but right now they were squawking up a storm and everyone was going to enjoy them and I was going to enjoy having enough customers, at least for one night.

CHAPTER 23

When I came back Cal Vachess had himself perched on top of a stool with one foot resting on another, spreading out his territory. He ordered a Jim Beam.

"So what brings you to Jacaranda?" I'd never told him my full name, hadn't mentioned the Sunset, so how had he found me? I came up with nothing except that Ryan thought he knew me. Maybe Ryan figured out why I was familiar or maybe Holly had told him about the Sunset, just as she'd told Sunny.

Cal winked at me and grinned. "It's a nice day for a drive. I thought I'd find out if you really wanted to come work for us."

"I'm not quite that desperate yet."

He tasted his drink and then set it back on the napkin. "How are you making out with finding that baby?"

"No luck with that either."

Cal was concentrating on his drink, turning it around with his fingers. "How old is this baby?"

Now I figured we were getting to why he had tracked me down. It was about Angel. "The baby's about nine months old."

The cash register pinged, telling me there was an order from out front. I was glad to escape from both the conversation and the man. Just how big a problem was Cal Vachess going to turn out to be? And how nasty?

While I worked on the order, Brian Spears came in and sat down on Cal's right and a conversation started up.

Cal turned out to have a wicked sense of humor and over the next hour he entertained everyone at the bar with circus stories. His patter was so well rehearsed it had to be something that he did often, but then he did stand out in a crowd and with the spotlight always on him, having stories to tell would be a good thing. How much of his stories were true was anyone's guess

"I grew up in Gibsonton, Florida, the circus-freak wintering town," Cal said. "The post office had a special counter for people of my size."

He gestured with his glass. "All the carnies spent the winter there. Like Melvin Burkhart, the human blockhead. He could hammer nails up his nose."

Brian drew back in shock. "Get out. If you drove a nail up your nose it would pierce your brain and kill you."

Cal spread his arms wide. "True story, I saw him do it; 'course, you have to remember he was a magician as well, so there might have been some sleight of hand involved, but it sure looked like that was what he was doing."

Brian held up his glass, signaling me for a refill. "What's Gibsonton like now? Maybe I'll go up and have a look."

"Oh, it's not near the fun it used to be. All the old guys are dying off and it's going upscale, getting cleaned up. They even closed the Giant's Camp Restaurant. But you should have seen Gibsonton when I was a kid. Everyone in town collected circus junk and stored it in the front yard. It was a point of pride to have the largest and most garish pile of rubbish."

I set down Brian's drink. "Sounds a little like the trailer park I grew up in. Unfortunately, there was no theme to our junk, nor rhyme or reason. The people in the Shoreline just liked junk."

An idea had been noodling around in my brain. Why would Cal ask how old Angel was unless he was trying to figure out when she was conceived? Cal might have known Holly better than he had let on and might have more interest in Holly than he pretended. Maybe, just maybe, the daddy of Holly's baby wasn't Dan. We only had Sunny's word that Holly wasn't seeing more than one man.

I was beginning to think there was a whole lot we didn't know about Holly. The happy young woman, chatty and friendly, had become someone I didn't recognize. Even Aunt Kay thought she was capable of selling her baby.

I was pouring a glass of wine when I had a glimpse of a new hell. Perhaps Cal already knew where Holly's baby was and he wanted to make sure I didn't find Angel. If Holly had given away or sold her baby, Cal Vachess might be the one who had Holly's baby. I tried not to think about what a purveyor of flesh would want with a little girl, pushed away all thoughts of what would happen to a child in his control. It was too ugly.

One thing was for certain. Whatever the reason Cal Vachess was in the Sunset, it didn't bode well for my earning easy money and leading a quiet life.

My cell started to whir. Normally I hate cell phones in my bar and glare hard at anyone holding one, but I'd left mine on. I looked at the display and said, "Hi."

Aunt Kay didn't waste time on hello, she just said, "Sunny called me. She was pretty upset."

"Why?"

"Cal Vachess came by to see her. Seems Sunny has the same reaction to him as you. She's terrified of him. She was really angry when she called me. She thought we'd told Cal her name and it took a while to make her believe me when I said we hadn't."

I moved out of earshot. "Holly again."

"That's what Sunny and I decided. Holly talked about everyone she knew."

"It was a problem at the Sunset. She'd be chatting when she should have been working." I glanced back at Cal, but he had his back to me, talking to Brian.

"Cal asked Sunny if she knew where to find Holly's baby." Aunt Kay asked the scary big question, "Why is he looking for Angel?"

"No idea."

"Do you suppose he thinks he's the father?"

"Or he thinks his brother is." I watched Cal, arms waving, as he recounted a tale. "Then again, maybe Cal sees this as a chance to pick up a little change."

A roar of laughter went up from Cal's listeners.

"Knowing where the baby is could be profitable," I said. "That's all he'd need to know to get interested."

Cal swiveled around to stare at me. I tried to smile before I turned my back to him. "What did Sunny tell Cal?"

"She said she told him nothing. She explained that she hadn't seen Holly and the baby after they moved out. I think Sunny can be close-mouthed when she wants to."

"No kidding." It brought a real smile to my lips. "Well, let's hope that's the end of it."

Through all the camaraderie and laughter, there was a tension about Cal, a taut wariness as if he were watching and waiting for something. I began to do the same, but the problem was I didn't know what I was waiting for.

I saw the change in Cal, saw him sit up a little straighter and grip the bar until his knuckles turned white. What he'd been waiting for had finally arrived. I followed his gaze to the door.

As if one Vachess wasn't bad enough, Ryan Vachess stood at the entrance. He was looking around as if he'd arrived at the zoo and he was trying to decide just which animal to study first.

I looked back to Cal to judge how worried I should be. Cal was on his feet, edgy and ready for action. His grim face told me all I needed to know. I swore under my breath. If his brother's arrival worried Cal, it sure as hell got my attention.

Ryan either didn't see Cal or was choosing to ignore him. But Ryan found me, standing behind the bar. A big grin spread across his face and he started for me. I debated moving away and letting Chris take care of Ryan, but experience has taught me that avoiding assholes seldom works.

When Ryan was in front of me, his dilated pupils showed he was either still high from this morning or was already tripping on something else. The second option would be better because coming down is when meth-heads are most dangerous, a time when they are to be avoided at all costs. Oh, yes, up was best.

I took a deep breath and reminded myself not to be confrontational, to just jolly him along. Too bad I never listen to my own advice.

Ryan said, "Bring me a scotch, sugar."

I placed the drink in front of him, picked up his twenty and went to turn away. He grabbed my hand and said, "I want to talk to you."

"I'm a little busy."

"Fine. I'll wait until you're done working." He gave me a confident smile. "It'll be better then. We can take our time."

I didn't even try and hide my disgust. "So, what brings you to the Sunset?"

Ryan took a deep drink of his scotch before he pointed the glass at me and said, "Holly told me all about you, told me about the Sunset. I had to see for myself."

"So now you've seen it." I went and got his change and dumped it on the bar in front of him.

"She had a real sweet picture of you. It took a minute, but as soon as you were out the door, I remembered you. I never forget a face, or a body. I remember yours."

"Lucky me."

"See, that's what I like about you. You got attitude."

"Enjoy your drink." I started to turn away but he called me back.

"You came to find me, remember? Holly and you both. Why?"

"You're wrong about that. I knew nothing about you until today. My Aunt Kay just wanted to understand what happened to Holly. That's why I came to see your brother Cal."

He wagged his finger at me and shook his head. "Holly and you were friends. It was me you wanted today."

"Holly worked for me as a waitress, we weren't particularly friends, and we didn't come looking for you, at least I didn't."

He leaned towards me. "I don't believe you."

"It was just a coincidence I met you today. They happen." I should have left it at that but instead I asked, "How did you meet Holly?"

"She said she called because of the name, Angel Photography, thought it was kismet, whatever the hell that is. She believed in fate and all kinds of shit like that." He put the glass of scotch over his heart in mock sincerity. "She just knew finding me was the right thing, knew this was the break she'd been looking for." The glass thumped on the bar. "She thought I was going to be her muse, make all her dreams come true. Where the hell did that come from? But she was sweet, all clingy and agreeable and incredible naive. That's why I dressed her in white, because that's how she was . . . pure, like life had never touched her."

"Guess that changed pretty quick after she met you. Not so sweet the way you treated her."

He scowled at me. "She liked it."

Any good sense I'd been born with disappeared with my rage. "And you liked using her and turning her into a prostitute."

He made a motion like cracking a whip. "I'm the circus master, controlling the action." His harsh laugh was too loud and brought a hush to the drinkers closest to him. They edged away.

I nodded to where Cal stood. "If you're ringmaster, what does that make Cal?"

Ryan's eyes sparkled. He was enjoying himself. "Oh, he's my dancing bear, dangerous and wild but on a leash."

"Well, why don't you take your pet bear and go home? The show is over."

And the fun was over for Ryan. The look he gave me was terrifying. Fear ate through my belly and crawled up my spine. I stepped back. But then he smiled and the horror seemed to disappear. He appeared truly delighted.

"We're going to be good together, you and I. A girl with attitude is a whole lot of fun."

It had been a long day and I don't react well to intimidation. My mouth slipped into drive before my brain was in gear. I leaned on the bar with both hands, wanting to spit in his face. "In the first place, I'm no girl. In the second place, my attitude precludes a guy like you."

Cal came up beside Ryan as I pointed to the door. "Have a good one."

Ryan's face twisted with outrage. His fist shot up, and for a second I thought he was going to punch me, but Cal was there, dragging down on his brother's arm with all of his weight, while I shot back away from him.

Around us the bar went silent. And then Ryan laughed. "Oh, you're fun."

He reached out with his left arm and picked up his drink and threw back the remainder of his scotch. "We're going to have fun, lots of dirty fun." He winked at me. "In the end, you'll call me sir."

"In your dreams, asshole."

"I'll remember that one," Ryan promised. He jerked his arm away from Cal and shrugged his jacket up around his shoulders and smoothed back his hair. "Oh, yes, I'll remember." He strolled to the door like he owned the world.

Cal said, "That wasn't a good idea."

"No kidding!"

"Stay away from Ryan. He's not coping with things too well right now."

"Ice and booze won't help his coping skills, and I wouldn't go near your brother with a ten-foot pole. Keep him out of my place."

Cal's bitter little laugh didn't lighten the mood. "I wish I could keep him out of a lot of places. Just stay away from him."

"Thing about a bar is people know where to find you."

CHAPTER 24

Violence leaves a residue that adheres like grease. Having friends and family say "It's over," doesn't help at all. It will never be over because death and brutality can't be put behind you like a bad dream.

Some days I hardly think about what happened to me in the past, about Jimmy's murder and being kidnapped by a psychopath, but every day I take precautions, habits that comfort me even if I don't acknowledge the need for them.

Even during the daylight hours I keep all the doors and windows locked and only the people closest to me know where I live. I always park directly under the light nearest the side door of the Sunset and I always make sure I don't stay at the restaurant after everyone else had gone. Anything left undone has to wait until morning.

Nights are my bad time. Taking martial arts, going to the shooting range and keeping pepper spray with me at all times hadn't added a thing to my sense of safety. Instead, they only made me feel more anxious, like I was preparing for the next time it happened, confirming a reason for my panic. For me no place feels safe anymore except when I'm behind the bar with a room full of people in front of me. Being alone, that's the worst and something I could never explain to Clay.

After the encounter with Ryan I went into my hunker-down-and-take-care mode, aware of every shadow and every possible hiding place as I left the Sunset. Once again, I had Miguel walk me to my pickup. The good thing about Miguel was that he never asked if it was necessary. If I asked him to stay with me or even follow me all the way home, that was good enough for Miguel. Tonight I asked him to follow me just as far as the south bridge.

The Sunset is on a barrier island, we call them keys in Florida, and it has a bridge to the mainland at the north end and another at the south. The only other access to Cypress Island is by boat. It should be the safest place in the world, but tonight it didn't feel like it. I locked the truck door as soon as it closed behind me and scanned the empty parking lot again, looking for Ryan's red Mustang.

As we headed south, a vehicle turned out of a public lot on the beach and pulled in behind Miguel. The roads were empty so Miguel had to be as aware of it as I was. Three vehicles now headed for the south bridge.

I reached for my cell to tell him to stay with me until I was safely home. The third set of lights disappeared. I dropped the phone back into my lap. Miguel's day had been just as long as mine.

There was just Miguel and me on the road now. At the bridge, Miguel hit his horn and made the left to go off the island. I tooted back and kept going south, down to the isolated beach house at the tip of the island. South Beach would never be my choice of a place to live. There was no street lighting on this stretch of the beach, and most of the houses were unoccupied in the off season. It was too remote and too unpopulated for me and I only stayed because I could live there for free.

Suddenly there were lights behind me again. They stayed well back, and didn't threaten me in any way, but I didn't like it. In the six months that I'd been traveling these roads at night I could count on one hand the number of times I'd met another vehicle.

I turned into the shell drive of the beach house and the suv went on by. Someone going home? I sat in the truck with the engine running and the lights off to see if they'd turn around and come back.

The drive was overgrown with thick underbrush on both sides, which kept any lights passing on the road from shining in towards the house. I'd only see the lights of another vehicle as they went by the end of the driveway. Nothing happened.

I checked out the house. It was well lit up. I don't go into dark houses anymore. I drove up as close as I could get to the house and waited some more.

The night was quiet. Even nature held her breath. I told myself that there was nothing to worry about, that the fear was all in my head, but I watched the rearview and stayed locked in the confines of the cab. Even though there was only glass to protect me, it felt safer there than running for the house and being exposed.

After ten minutes no lights had appeared at the end of the drive. No one had followed me home.

I turned off the engine and ran for the kitchen door with my keys in my hand. But even inside with the door locked I didn't feel safe.

I drew the drapes and left on all the lights, in the living room, the halls, second bedroom and bath. The only room with no light on was the kitchen because there were no window coverings there. A lit room without curtains makes me feel like a target.

But I was alone. Sleep was a long way off so I opened the bottle of Chardonnay I'd brought from the restaurant and settled down in front of the tv. The late movie was *The Sound and the Fury*, with Joanne Woodward and Yul Brynner, a story about another dysfunctional Southern family. "See, it could be worse" is sort of a mantra for me.

It was after one when I put the half-empty bottle of wine in the fridge. In the pale light from the hall, I rechecked the kitchen door and went cautiously to the window over the sink and tested the catch. The clasp was so wobbly a stray termite could break in and I'd promised myself for months that it was something that I'd get fixed. Tomorrow for sure.

Leaning on the sink, I stared out into the darkness beyond the faint glow seeping from the light on the carport. In the silence, the refrigerator wheezed and ice dropped into the bucket.

I studied the night, not really looking for anything, more as a ritual to reassure myself.

And then a light, where no light should be, appeared at the road, briefly . . . for a second only . . . and then it was gone. What kind of a light was it? The only thing I could think of was the light from a cell phone of someone out walking late at night. But it was too late for a stroll and too late to be making a normal call. I'd been traveling these roads for months and had never seen anyone out walking after dark.

I clutched the edge of the sink, every muscle straining, watching for the light to return. I told myself I was mistaken. Too many times lately I'd seen danger where there was none, cried wolf and had to apologize. This was just one more product of my overactive imagination. None of that stopped my panic. I waited. Only darkness.

Telling myself it was my head playing tricks on me didn't stop the terror. Grabbing up my purse, I ran for the bedroom, taking out the pepper spray as I went and slamming the bedroom door shut behind me. I wedged the toe of a shoe under the bottom edge of the door and then I shoved a chest of drawers in front of it before I got Clay's revolver out of the closet and fed six rounds into the cylinder.

I flicked off the light. Separating the curtains with a finger, I peered outside. It was a bright moonlit night. The dunes cast long shadows, deep pools of blackness for concealment, while drifts of sand and clumps of beach grasses offered more hiding places. I watched for movement. The breeze off the water waved the grasses, but other than that everything was still. Then something rustled in the clump of palms growing at the corner of the house. I lifted the Smith & Wesson, took a deep breath and let it out slowly, bracing my gun hand with my left just as I had been taught to do when preparing to shoot. And then I waited for a target to appear.

A coon ran through the shaft of moonlight from the house to the nearest dune.

I stepped away from the window and lowered the gun. I gently placed the gun on top of the night table. My hands were trembling and my whole body was reacting to the release of fear.

Sleep was gone. I huddled in the bed, clutching my cell in one hand and my canister of pepper spray in the other hand. Rationally, I knew no one was out in the dark stalking me, but it's hard to be sensible in the middle of the night.

I hit Clay's number.

"Hi, darlin'," he drawled, as though it were two in the afternoon and not two in the morning.

"I can't sleep." I didn't even bother apologizing about the time. He'd heard it all before.

"Tell me," he said softly, as if it were the first time.

"I saw a light where no light should be and I think someone followed me back from the Sunset."

"Want me to come home?" It was the same offer he always made when I called late at night, no matter that he'd already told me he couldn't come home.

I loosened my grip on the can of hot pink pepper spray and laid it on the bed. I rolled on my side. "Talking to you makes me feel better. I'm okay during the day but not at night."

I pulled the edge of the spread over me. "Will I ever get over these panic attacks? Will I ever believe that it's over?"

"God, Sherri, after what you've been through? It isn't something you put behind you like a parking ticket. It'll take time and some help."

"You help me."

"I mean professional help."

"Let's not start that again. I don't need anyone else but you."

He didn't answer, didn't give me any reassurance or say he'd always be there to look after me.

The night had just become longer.

CHAPTER 25

Somewhere around four I drifted off and awoke about eight to the sound of a chainsaw. I was out of bed and on my feet, hunting for a weapon before I identified the enemy. With my heart still racing, I slowly realized that no one was coming through the walls to get at me. It was the beginning of the renovations on the house next door.

Light flooded through the thin curtains. Daylight took away most of my anxiety but still I crept through the house with the pepper spray in my hand, waiting for someone to jump out at me. I was more than prepared to cause the temporary blindness, choking and nausea the manufacturer promised.

I wished I'd also bought the stun gun, for twenty-seven dollars and ninety-nine cents, which was on special when I bought the spray. One more night like the last one and a stun gun was going to be a mandatory part of my arsenal. My ways of coping with my terror might be ratcheting up my feelings of panic rather than diminishing them, but they had the advantage of being affordable and immediate. Nothing says safe like a stun gun.

And all because of a light, a tiny little firefly of a light that I saw for maybe ten seconds. Maybe Marley and Clay were right and I was a card-carrying member of the crazy party and it was time to get professional help. Even knowing what I feared was all in my head didn't offer any relief. Bummer.

I went for a short run, wearing my pepper spray, my can of comfort, in a little tube container around my neck. It did more to make me feel secure than any therapist ever could.

When I switched on my cell there were calls from Marley and Clay, but it was the voicemail from my former mother-in-law, saying, "Let's do lunch and talk things out," that had me hyperventilating.

"Yeah, when hell freezes over, bitch," I screamed at my cell.

I could wipe away her voice but not the burning anger that shot through me. I had a stock of things that would bring me joy to tell Bernice, a long list of stuff I'd been holding onto since I first met her, but there was no way I was going to risk losing what Aunt Kay was paying me by taking time off. Still, there was one small, mean way to get even. After my shower, I called Bernice and told her I would meet her for lunch. Leaving Bernice sitting there, waiting for me to show up, would be almost as sweet as telling the bitch a few colorful truths.

Aunt Kay opened the door and stepped back into the kitchen. "Did you find out why Cal was in Jacaranda?"

"Well, good morning to you to."

She frowned.

I closed the door and took a good look at her. She was dressed in pink . . . hot pink. Her cropped pink pants were topped with a square-cut pink top emblazoned with a pink sequined flamingo. In a crowd I'd be able to find her. She flashed like neon.

I said, "I'm not sure what either of them wanted."

"Either?"

"Yup, Vachess times two."

"Oh dear." Her forehead wrinkled in thought. "Was it just a coincidence that they came to the Sunset?"

"Please."

She pulled out a chair and sat down. "How did they know where to find you?"

"The same way Sunny knew. Holly told them about me, although why she talked about me, I'll never know."

"Let's face it, your life has been more exciting than most. Make a guess why they came to the Sunset."

"Ryan was still high and thought I came to Sarasota searching for him. Maybe he was excited by the thought of a woman hunting for him, some kind of sexual turn on."

"And Cal, why was he there?"

"Cal seemed to know Ryan was going to show up at the Sunset and was there to try to control him. That's what I made of it, but maybe I got it wrong."

She nodded her head, thinking it through. "So it wasn't about Holly?"

"I'm not sure." I took a deep breath. "This is the bottom line. I don't want anything to do with those guys, Aunt Kay." I could see the Sunset going down the tubes as I said it. "They're out of our league."

She straightened. "We'll stay well away from them, but I still want to see if we can find Angel, okay? That's all I'm interested in."

"Fine. But if we seem to be crossing into their territory, I'm done. Agreed?"

"Agreed." She picked up her purse and got to her feet, waving me towards the door. "Now let's go."

The name of the lawyer was Shane Deveral. It took a little talking on Aunt Kay's part to get him to see us without an appointment. When he heard why we were there, he suggested, none too politely, that we leave.

Aunt Kay heaved a resigned sigh and said, "All right, dear."

"Oh, oh," I said to myself. I'd worked out that when Aunt Kay said "dear" like that, what she was really saying to Shane was, "All right, asshole, this is where I get tough."

"All right, dear," she said again to old Shane, "I didn't want to turn this over to the police. I wanted to keep it all quiet and casual, as it were. I just want to know where Angel is, but perhaps the police need to know about your work here. Maybe they need to look into the adoptions you handle."

"Don't be silly," Shane said.

I could have cautioned him not to diss Aunt Kay, but I hadn't warmed to old Shane. Let him find out for himself.

He said, "Everything is perfectly legal."

"I'm sure it is," Aunt Kay said sweetly. "I'm not one to complain, but I did hear a rumor." She turned to me. "Sherri, what was the name of that friend of yours who bought a baby?"

Shane looked like a wolverine had just clamped down on his testicles.

"Wasn't the lawyer that arranged it a Mr. Deveral too?" She swung around to study him. "Well, perhaps bought is too strong a word, but there was a lot of money involved."

She leaned towards Shane. "My nephew is in the district attorney's office. I'm sure he would be interested enough to help his auntie out."

Aunt Kay didn't have any family but I figured I'd keep that to myself.

Shane's eye twitched. Not much, but the twitch hadn't been there when we came in.

"Everything is by the book," he said.

"What book would that be, dear?" Aunt Kay's voice was louder and more demanding when she said, "What was the name of you friend, Sherri?"

Before I needed to deliver an answer Shane lifted his palms and said, "Okay, no need to bring others into it. Yes, Holly Mitchell got in touch with me and asked if I could find a nice family for her baby. I did. But Holly never went through with it." His handsome features twisted. "Left me with a real problem."

"Did she say why she changed her mind?"

"Not exactly. She brought the baby in when the couple were here and showed them her little girl. She didn't know the adopting family's name but they all seemed happy enough with their agreement. Everything was fine, a done deal, but they wanted the baby to have a complete physical before they signed the papers. I made the appointment. It was for three days later. The day after the doctor's appointment, Holly was supposed to bring in the baby and turn her over to her new parents. Holly didn't show up. When I called her, she just said something silly like she wasn't going to let a man like that raise her child. She said she found out he was using some escort service. I'm not sure where she got that idea, but I couldn't talk her out of it. I never saw her or the baby again, didn't even talk to her again. Now if you don't mind, I have a practice to run."

"Yes, dear, a very valuable one I'm sure," Aunt Kay said. "Now if you could just give me his name, the name of this man who wanted to adopt Holly's baby."

Shane was beyond outraged. "No way. That's confidential."

Aunt Kay said, "I suppose you found this couple another child, even after you knew about the escort service. I'm not sure that would disqualify him but . . ." She left the sentence unfinished. "Do you know Sean Contrell, the district attorney in Sarasota? Such a nice boy, always my favorite nephew."

All these years I'd been blaming Tully Jenkins and his family for my lying ways, but maybe my inspiration had come from another source.

"I'm sure Sean could clarify if you acted irresponsibly in finding them another baby. And I'm sure Sean could find Holly's baby for me. But I do hate to disturb him."

Shane clenched his jaw, grinding money for his dentist.

"You don't have to write it down," Aunt Kay told him. "I have a very good memory, and no one will ever know where I got the name and address from." She looked up at me and smiled. "If it ever comes up I'll say it came from Holly. It will be fine."

"Gary and Melissa Hunt. He owns Elegant Dressing."

Aunt Kay pushed herself to her feet, a queen in hot pink. She didn't thank him and didn't say goodbye. I followed her out of the office like a good little puppy dog.

CHAPTER 26

Elegant Dressing is a premier clothing store in Sarasota, representing all the big name designers, and selling both women's clothes and men's. Clay had brought me here to buy what he called "the one good suit" that everyone apparently needs in their wardrobe. Turned out that the bank was unimpressed by my black suit and they still wanted their money.

Gary Hunt was about forty, slim and impeccably dressed in a charcoal suit with a pink striped tie. Now even faux pearls give me hives, and I'll never be into dressing like a member of the Christian Right at a Republican convention, but still I wished I'd been wearing my funeral suit instead of black jeans, a tee-shirt and flip-flops. He was just so perfect. And he was also beyond annoyed with us. He knew we didn't belong in a store like his, could tell we weren't there to buy a good suit.

I watched a master at work with awe and amazement. It didn't take Aunt Kay long to sort Gary out. If a room of screaming kids didn't scare her there was no way this supercilious ass was going to accomplish it. He sure tried, though. Within five minutes she had him thinking she was either on the way to the police or else she was there to blackmail him. I wasn't sure which of those scenarios she was actively working on and neither was he, but he wasn't taking any chances by pissing her off. He quickly decided he needed to chat with us in the privacy of his office.

Aunt Kay followed him past the counters of cashmere sweaters and Gucci loafers as though it were stuff waiting for a Goodwill truck. She didn't care that she should be wearing a good suit instead of hot pink.

The office was all dark shiny wood and the desk was covered in open books of material samples. Gary didn't ask us to sit down. "I was never told that girl's name. I just walked into the hotel room and knew she was the mother of the little girl we were supposed to adopt."

"And Holly didn't like you being a john," I said.

He flushed. "Yeah, well she was in the room too, selling what I was buying, so what made her so high and mighty?"

Aunt Kay waved his words aside. "What happened next?"

"She told me I was never going to get her child and ran out of the room."

"And of course you called Cal and complained," I said.

He turned to look at me. His nose twitched like he'd caught a bad smell. "I called Angel Escort and told them I wasn't happy with their service. It took them an hour to send over a replacement for that girl, one well below my normal standards. I haven't used their service since."

"Poor you." My sarcasm was lost on him.

Aunt Kay was focused on finding out about Holly. "And you never saw or heard from Holly again?"

"No. I wanted no part of a crazy woman like her."

He shouldn't have said that in a tone of righteous indignation like he was the injured party. It made me want to strike him, to hurt him bad so I left him with something to worry over. "W-e-l-l," I drew the word out like I was really uncertain, "I hope it won't be necessary to bring you into it . . . with the police and everything. You see, Holly is dead and questions are being asked, but I'm sure you have nothing to be concerned about."

I walked to the door and then turned back as if I remembered something. "And that private detective the family hired, I'm sure he'll be discreet. He just wants to find the men Holly was involved with." Why should I be the only one up at nights worrying? "I hope your wife won't be too upset. And . . . well, never mind, no one will likely be charged for that so you won't have to testify."

He made a strangling sort of noise. I didn't stop to see if he was merely expressing an opinion or having a stroke. I didn't care much either way.

Aunt Kay joined me by the tie counter, linking her arm in mine and beaming up at me like a master who was proud of a star student.

We stepped out into the heat.

"To think, that shit intimidated me when Clay and I went in to buy my suit."

Aunt Kay opened her eyes wide in mock surprise. "I didn't think anyone could intimidate you."

"I just bluster louder and swear more when people are getting to me."

She laughed. "Oh, right. In that case I've seen you intimidated." Her smile faded. "You know what this means, don't you?"

"Sure, but tell me anyway."

"Cal Vachess knew about the child, although he told us he didn't. When Mr. Hunt called in outrage to complain, I'm sure he mentioned Holly's baby."

"Could be. Or maybe Gary Hunt just complained that the girl the escort service sent ran out on him. He wouldn't want them to know anything personal."

She halted. "Sherri, remember Holly told Sunny she gave Angel to friends? Friends might mean high school for Holly. She doesn't seem to have made many friends since. If there was anyone closer to her than Sunny, they would have been driving her to appointments. And if she needed someone to look after Angel, wouldn't she go back to the people she knew?"

"She did go back to people she knew. She came to you."

"But where did she go after I said I couldn't take Angel? She never came to you?"

"Don't you think I'd have mentioned it if she had? Besides, I wouldn't be anyone's idea of a mother substitute."

"So who is it? Who did she take Angel to?"

"Maybe her parents."

Aunt Kay shook her head. "I don't think so. Remember, her mother knew nothing about a baby when I saw her in May."

Then she said, "I wish I could see Hannah."

She sighed. "I suppose our next stop should be Marnie Mitchell. We'll see her after lunch." Her voice left no room for dissent. "I have to go to the hospital for a test. You can drop me off there and go find a yearbook from Holly's class while I'm gone."

"Bernice asked me to have lunch with her."

"Oh." The surprise was clear on her face. "Wait a minute, we have a deal, and this week is mine."

"Even slaves are allowed to eat."

"Are you really going to have lunch with her?"

"There are a few suggestions I'd like to make to Bernice."

"Okay." It was reluctant and then she added, "Wait until after my test and then I'll come with you."

"No. This isn't going to be a Hallmark moment and you don't want to hear what I've got to say to her."

"Yes I do."

I laughed. "Not going to happen," I said, although she'd probably enjoy our shit-slinging fest a whole lot. "You find out where Holly's parents are and when they can see us. I'll pick you up after I deal with Bernice."

CHAPTER 27

I dropped Aunt Kay off and went back to the beach house to put on my dragon-slayer outfit. Forty minutes later I checked myself out in the mirror and said, "Hello, Mamma." There she was, my mother, Ruth Ann Jenkins, wearing a leopard print top that crossed in front of her breasts and a skin-tight black leather skirt that was a little too short to be polite. To heighten the impact and make sure nothing important was overlooked a wide red belt separated the leather from the leopard. But best of all were the red leather stilettos with the platform soles. They brought me to my ideal height of six feet. Trashy but sexy is the look I do best.

Damn, I looked good . . . like a transvestite on the way to a gay bar for happy hour! My Chinese-red painted lips kissed the image in the mirror. "Welcome back." I checked out the view from the rear. "Coming and going, you'll give the bitch a heart attack."

I stopped just inside the door of the restaurant and let the full impact of my outfit hit her.

Bernice didn't faint and she didn't spew out her disgust when I sat down across from her. That was a big disappointment. I could only hope that the pressure built up from holding all the venom in would rupture something vital.

She picked up the menu and said, "Let's have the tuna. Jimmy loved it. Remember?"

Remember? The only way I could forget would be to cut off my head.

The waiter scurried over to our table. "Would you like a drink to start?"

What in hell was the fool talking about? I'd need a bucketful of booze if I was going to sit across from Bernice for an hour and not turn homicidal.

Bernice looked at me and raised an eyebrow.

I gave him my brightest smile. "Why don't you just bring by a bottle of Glenlivet and a bucket of ice and I'll take care of it from there?"

The waiter looked startled. He turned to Bernice for help.

She said, "Bring her a Chardonnay." Then she ordered the grilled tuna for both of us. She waited until our server left before saying, "Still have your little vice, I see."

"What little vice would that be?"

"Oh, you know what I'm talking about."

"Without my little vice I'd have no hobby."

"More like no reason to live." Bernice may have plumped up, but she hadn't lost her edge.

"I didn't come here to discuss my drinking habits." I looked away from her, trying to get my emotions under control. I couldn't let her win this soon in our scrimmage.

"They have karaoke here on Thursday nights," I said. "I think hell probably comes with karaoke."

"Yes, karaoke that only has Barry Manilow songs." The silver bangles on her arm jangled as she lifted her glass of water. "Your father makes me happy."

"Your happiness is not high on my totem pole."

I took my first good look at her. Dr. Travis, Jimmy's father, was a plastic surgeon and his wife had benefited greatly from his profession.

I hated to admit it, but she looked ten years younger than the age on her birth certificate.

She drummed long red talons on the white tablecloth and considered me. She said, "All right, how about this—I make your father happy."

"He's always had low standards."

The waiter set two glasses of wine on the table. I picked up my glass and took a very healthy swallow. Alcohol was all that was standing between me and killing the bitch.

A smug smile teased Bernice's lips, as if I'd just proven her point.

I set the glass down, although I wanted to drain it, and I locked my fingers together in my lap. "I thought the thing this year was younger men. There are lots of them around and most of them aren't too discriminating when you have as much money as you do."

"Oh, I tried one," she said, all playful and pleased, "but he was a disappointment. The sex was great but he insisted on talking."

"That can be so annoying. Perhaps you didn't tip him enough."

We stirred our pot of hate, each adding a little hot pepper of cruelty and made sure it was still simmering, until at last she leaned forward and said, "Don't screw this up for me. Play nice and I promise you won't regret it."

"That will be a first!" The waiter came with a basket of rolls. I waited for him to leave before I added, "Regrets are all I ever got from the Travis family." I wasn't sipping the Chardonnay anymore.

Bernice leaned back in her chair. "So why did you keep the name?"

"Prettier than Jenkins and it gave you a bucketful of pain." I picked up my glass. It was empty. I looked around. Where the hell had the waiter disappeared to? The place was almost empty and there wasn't a waiter in sight. What did I have to do to get another drink?

"Why Tully?" I asked, really curious about this. "He's the kind of guy who gives rednecks a bad name."

She pulled away in mock surprise. "Don't talk about your daddy that way. I've convinced him to stop scratching in public." She smiled. It was a genuine smile, an unnerving sight and not one I was used to seeing on Bernice. "I won't talk about love, you wouldn't believe me if I did. I've been alone for a long time, alone in a marriage that died well before Jimmy did, but his death finished it." Again that freaky smile. "I knew there was nothing left the day I walked in on my husband and his new nurse. She's a lovely girl, very perky and alert. Just like her tits. When I saw them, the tits I mean, I recognized James's handiwork at once. Implants must be a new employee benefit. The strange thing was I didn't care anymore." She picked up her water glass and laughed. "I ran into Tully about an hour later."

Too bad she hadn't run into a semi instead. "Fate plays such cruel tricks."

"I wish it had been ten years ago. What a waste being unhappy is."

She cocked her head to the side. "When are you going to start a family? It's all your dad talks about."

"I'm too busy staying alive to have a kid."

"You might like having a little thing living in the house with you."

"Fine, I'll let the mold grow in the shower."

"Well, all I'm saying is you're just about past your sell-by date."

"That's more like it," I said to her. "I knew the real Bernice couldn't stay gone for long."

"Well, you know the true me, that's for sure. You always bring out my best, but you're pretty quick to stick the blade in as well." She tipped her water glass towards me in a salute. "Not as skillful as me, of course."

"You're right. I never was in your league. Never could be the bitch you are."

Our tuna arrived and I gave up on the second drink.

On the way out the door we met two guys coming in. The first guy, short and stocky but dressed for success, took one look at me and said, "Woo, Momma, I think I'm in love."

I planted my fist on my hip and asked, "You think you can handle this?"

"I'm willing to die trying," he vowed, and he sincerely looked like he meant it.

When the door closed behind us, I tipped my sunglasses down and said to Bernice, "See, that's why I dress like this."

"Oh," she said, nodding in understanding. "And here I thought it was because you're a slut."

Down, and playing from well behind, I headed for the truck, digging out my jumble of keys from my bag.

Bernice called, "And when are you going to get rid of that stupid pickup?"

I opened the door and threw my bag on the passenger seat. I pointed the ignition key at her. "When you get rid of that ridiculous blonde football helmet you wear."

Her right hand started for her hair before she caught herself. Still losing and well behind but picking up points, I wiggled my butt up onto the seat before she thought of a comeback.

CHAPTER 28

There's a big secret that people in the service industry all know. If you really want to dig up the dirt on someone, ask the person who changes their sheets and does their wash. If you want to spy, ask the person who empties their trash and tidies their desk. Never mind their friends. They only know what they're meant to hear; it's the people in the service industry who have all the good stuff. I knew a guy working in a bar on Siesta Key who brags he's got the dirt on everyone of note living in the county.

My run in with Cal and Ryan had left me trembling. While I hoped I'd seen the last of them, experience said there was more to come. I needed to know all I could about them, needed to know how to protect myself. I headed for the Clam Shack to see Sammy.

"Holy jumping Judas, be still my aching heart." Sammy Defino spread his arms wide in welcome. "My dreams have come true at last."

"Now don't go getting my hopes up, Sammy, you know Ilsa won't let you out at night." I slid up onto a barstool and dropped my shoulder bag on another one.

He screwed his face up into mock misery. "It's true. She's never been the understanding type."

We shared a laugh and commiserated on business before I asked if he knew Ryan Vachess.

Sammy threw his arms in the air. "Christ, don't go fucking with that psycho."

"I don't want anything to do with him, far from it."

"Then why are you asking?" He didn't wait for an answer. "Those brothers are pond scum, dangerous and nasty guys, and that Ryan is one sick freak."

Sammy glanced at a couple of men in suits further down the bar and bent closer to me, whispering, "People they don't like disappear."

"I just want to keep him away from me and I need any information I can get on how to do that."

"Then go out to St. Armand's and talk to Rob McCabe. His sister got mixed up with Vachess and was never seen again."

"Thanks, Sammy." I slid off the stool. "Why don't you and Ilsa come down on your night off and I'll treat you to a meal."

"Ah, Sherri, I'd love to, but Ilsa won't let me near you since I told her you were the girl who taught me to French kiss."

"Jesus, Sammy, she can't hold that against me. I did my best to teach you but I can't help it if you're a slow learner."

Keys stretch along the west coast of Florida like the backbone of some giant beast rising out of the gulf. Back in the 1920s, John Ringling, the circus guy, bought a group of those keys and today the hottest real estate in all Florida is on those islands.

I took the John Ringling Causeway over Sarasota Bay to Lido Key, famous for its white sand, as fine as sugar.

St. Armand's Circle, where Rob McCabe owned a deli, is the jewel in the crown of Lido Key. Parking on St. Armand's is a dog-eat-dog type of situation with cars going around and around the loop, waiting for a space to open up and blocking traffic when someone is spotted who looks like he might be leaving. The driver parks in the middle of traffic with his blinker on, ignoring the honks of cars jamming up behind him, while a shopper puts things in the trunk. Most times he's disappointed and the whole thing starts over again, like motorized musical chairs.

I got lucky and snagged a parking spot on the street nearly in front of the deli.

The half-dozen tables outside the McCabe Bakery & Deli were all filled with people sharing gossip and coffee. A long line of waiting customers blocked the door and glared at me as I slipped by them. Inside, the display cases were filled with cheesecakes and pastries, a choice of a dozen salads, and any kind of sandwich you could ever dream up.

There was only one man behind the counter. He was taking orders and slapping sandwiches together without a smile or a word for his customers, like a man who hadn't had a good day in a long time. In his late thirties, he had thinning, sand-colored hair and two deep vertical furrows between his eyebrows.

When there was a break in the action I asked him if he was Rob McCabe. He nodded and I told him who I was and why I was there.

Color came into his cheeks when he heard Ryan Vachess's name. He stood straighter and his jaw hardened. "Follow me." He pulled off his white-bibbed apron and threw it from him and then he plunged through a curtained exit without waiting for me.

I went to the end of the deli case and slipped behind the counter saying, "Excuse me," to two women who stopped serving and gave me curious looks. I followed Rob through a tiny storage room and out to the alley where the air smelled of the hot pavement and the garbage in the dumpsters.

I was barely outside when Rob McCabe turned on me, his face contorted with rage and hatred. "That bastard. You're crazy if you have anything to do with him."

I stepped away. "Look, I just want to know how to protect myself from this guy."

"Shoot him would be my suggestion." He pulled a package of cigarettes out of his breast pocket. "Why do you want to know about Vachess?"

I told him about Holly and then I added, "Now tell me how you know him."

"Chloe was my half-sister." He dragged smoke deep into his lungs. "Two years ago, when she was eighteen and just out of high school and full of beans, she met Ryan Vachess." He dragged hungrily on the cigarette and then dropped the butt on the pavement, toeing it out even as his hand reached for another one. "Within a month she was living with him."

"The last time I saw her she was with Vachess outside a dance club in Tampa and she was high as a kite on something. I tried to drag her into my car. I got arrested and I never saw her again." He hunched his shoulders and stubbed the pavement with the toe of his shoe.

"I went to the police. Nothing ever came of it. They said she was an adult and could do as she wanted. The police listed her as a runaway but honest to god she wouldn't have gone away from us and never gotten in touch. It wasn't like that; we were a good family. It nearly killed my dad and stepmother." He wrinkled his face, holding back his feelings.

"They're still waiting for her to walk through the door but I know she's dead."

Sorry is too small a word for something like that, so I didn't offer it.

"I've tried the police, put up flyers, attempted to track Chloe on the Internet, and none of it was worth rat shit. It's not knowing, that's the worst. A couple of times a week I have to watch that bastard walking past the deli, going to lunch down at the Cuban restaurant with another young fool, and there isn't anything I can do about it."

A seagull clattered onto the closed top of a dumpster, walked across the lid and then rose screeching into the air when Rob waved his arm at it.

"The only thing that keeps me from killing the bastard is the fact that my parents need me. I'm all they've got left. They couldn't stand to lose me too."

A delivery van started down the alley and we stepped back inside to get out of its way.

"Did you know Ryan is using?"

"He's more than using. He's the biggest dealer in town. Painkillers, party drugs, whatever the market wants. A cop told me he's got people cooking meth for him up and down the gulf coast. Seems they can make meth in the back of vans now and just keep moving from place to place."

My chest constricted in panic. "He's worse than I thought."

"The Vachess brothers deal in women and drugs and they have money and connections. They're dangerous," Rob said. "You be careful."

"Trust me, I intend to be."

"If you hear anything about our Chloe, will you let me know?"

"Of course, but it's unlikely to happen."

"I know, but I have to ask. Here . . ." Rob went to a wooden desk, shoved up against boxes of paper napkins. He opened a manila envelope and pulled out a sheet of paper. He held it out to me.

I looked down at a picture of a laughing young woman. Under it was her information and Rob McCabe's name and telephone number. I wondered where he was going to get the fifty-thousand-dollar reward he was offering.

"Just in case . . ." He couldn't finish.

I guess he still had hope despite what he'd said.

CHAPTER 29

Aunt Kay was waiting out in front of the hospital when I pulled up. It must have been a hundred and twenty degrees on the concrete. She was sweating like a cold glass of beer beside a hot grill, but there she stood.

"Why didn't you wait inside?"

"I didn't know you were going to be so late, did I?" The curb gave her enough height to heft her behind onto the seat without my help, but the exertion left her breathless.

She didn't ask about my time with Bernice. Imagine that. Instead she said, "We're going over to see Marnie Mitchell. I called her while I was hanging around waiting for you. She's over on Lime."

As I waited for a delivery truck to pull out in front of me I said, "What was in that note Holly left behind?"

"Why are you asking?"

"Curious. Maybe there's something in it that will tell us where to look for Angel."

"No, there wasn't anything that would help."

"So how come you don't want to tell me what it said?"

"Don't go making a big deal of it."

"I think you're the one that's making it a big deal, turning it into a mystery. Just tell me."

Aunt Kay sighed. "All right." But it took her a while to get the words out. "The note said, 'because my Angel is gone and I can't live

140

without my Angel. I have no home and no one to look after me. I have nothing left. This is the only way.'"

"And you thought . . ." But, I couldn't put it into words what she thought might have happened to Angel.

Aunt Kay nodded. "I think Angel might be dead."

A car honked and I jerked the truck back into my own lane.

"She said Angel was gone." The words were almost whispered, as if to say her fears out loud would make them true. "I want to know for sure if Angel is dead and if she is, I want to know why."

I could hardly take in what Aunt Kay was saying. "Do you think . . . ?" I took a deep breath and started over. "What do you think happened?"

"It's just that . . ." She couldn't go on. "Why didn't Marnie Mitchell know about the baby?"

"If Holly gave up her baby for adoption, she wouldn't tell anyone, would she?"

"I hope you're right." She sighed. "Holly was never strong."

"Can you remember exactly what the note said?"

She made a noise of disgust. "I'm not likely to forget it, am I?"

I had ample opportunity to know about Aunt Kay's amazing memory. In grade seven, she'd caught me out in a forged note from my mother. She knew the handwriting of every parent and every teacher. No one fooled her. The note had to be written by Holly or been a damn good copy or Aunt Kay would know.

I pulled into a parking space along the street and got an old envelope out of the glove compartment and handed it to her along with a pencil. "Write it down."

When she was finished she handed me the note. Despite his confidence, I thought Dan might have made a mistake but what had bothered me about Dan's copy of Holly's suicide note was there on Aunt Kay's—the same strange opening. Why? I stuffed it in my bag so I could compare them. "You must have a reason for thinking Angel is dead."

"Holly's note was filled with such despair." Aunt Kay rubbed her forehead. "Something awful happened to her and Angel being dead makes as much sense as Holly killing herself."

"Well, I think Angel is somewhere safe and I'm going to find her." I pulled around a semi making a turn. "Holly wouldn't let anything bad happen to Angel. If Holly didn't care she would have let the Hunts adopt her baby."

"Yes, that's true, isn't it?" For a moment she seemed all hopeful, but that was wiped away by her next words. "But what would Holly do if her mind was disturbed? And it must have been unbalanced for her to kill herself."

"Look, Holly was a sweet person, not too . . . well, sensible, but kind and good."

"That's the Holly you knew."

I glanced over at Aunt Kay. There were things about Holly, secrets that she wasn't going to tell, that were coloring her view of events.

"How do you explain the Holly that became a sex worker?" she said. "I would have thought she'd never have done anything like that."

Aunt Kay turned to me, her mouth open to continue her argument. Instead, she gave a soft, "Oh," and then she asked, "Is that what you wore to your lunch?"

"Yes."

"Interesting choice."

I didn't answer.

She turned away and said, "Take the next left and we can cut across on Harvard."

"I know how to get there."

"Yes, dear, of course you do."

"Ah, the asshole thing again."

"What?"

"Dear—it's what you call people instead of calling them an asshole like I would."

She slapped her knees and laughed, but she didn't disagree with me.

"When I called Marnie Mitchell, I asked about Holly's friends from high school but she didn't seem to know any. I asked her to write down any names she remembered so we could get in touch with them for Holly's memorial."

"Holly's memorial?"

"Didn't I mention that?"

I turned onto Lime and she said, "I know you said we should stay away from that escort service, but I think you have to go back and talk to Mr. Vachess again."

"No way. Some guys pretend to be tough, but Cal Vachess is the real deal. He doesn't carry that gun just for show and I'm pretty sure that if he wanted you crippled he knows just the guys to do it for him. You don't survive in the business he's in if you aren't prepared to play rough. Forget him."

"But how will we find out about Holly?"

I hated the pain and defeat in her voice.

"I doubt he knows anything, and even if he did, he wouldn't tell us. He's out of our league. Let's just leave it at that and hope we never meet up with him again."

"If he doesn't know anything about Holly or Angel, why was he interested enough to go to the Sunset last night?"

"I don't know, and trust me I've spent a lot of time thinking about it. All I know is that I want him to go away and forget he knows my name. Forget he knows where to find me."

"Oh dear, I guess I shouldn't have called him."

While I was screaming, "You did what?" at Aunt Kay, I nearly drove into the back of a garbage truck. When things settled down and my heart rate was almost normal, I said, "Say that again."

"I called him."

"Shit. Why?"

"Well, you took so long to come back and the payphone was right there. After I talked to Marnie I just thought I'd see if he'd tell me anything more than he told you. Holly worked for him months ago when she met Gary Hunt, and then Dan found a call from the escort service on her phone from Saturday. What was she doing in between? Was she still working for them? It doesn't make sense."

"What did Vachess say?"

"He wasn't there. That's a good thing, isn't it?"

"Did you leave your name and number?"

"Yes."

I blew out a long breath, trying to think it through. "What exactly did you say? Did you mention me?"

She nodded. Watching me closely, she said, "I told him I was your aunt and that I had some more questions about Holly. I guess I shouldn't have called."

Did Aunt Kay's call make the situation worse? One way or another, he knew more about me than I was comfortable with, but hopefully he'd just delete Aunt Kay's message and that would be an end to it.

I stopped believing in fairy tales a long time ago.

CHAPTER 30

Marnie Mitchell lived in a crumbling apartment building out by the airport—a faded yellow building, where maintenance was kept to a bare minimum. Tall pines dwarfed the two-storey structures and all the screened porches across the front were in tatters or missing.

"It's so good of you to come." Mrs. Mitchell stepped aside so we could enter the tiny furnished apartment put together from the left-overs of someone else's life. The air smelled of her flowery perfume, and the sounds of a crying child and the laugh track from a sitcom intruded from next door.

She pointed to a tiny sitting area. "Please sit down."

I edged around the coffee table and slumped down into the couch. The springs had gone from under the brown Naugahyde and if Aunt Kay joined me I'd need a crane to get her out. Aunt Kay wisely opted for turning around a straight-back chair from the tiny dinette set.

Mrs. Mitchell sat on the floral loveseat across from me, knees together and back rigid. She was an older version of Holly, like an aged ghost of the person I knew, the same face, build and bone structure. Most of all she used her hands just like Holly. They were never still, always reaching out to touch something before changing their mind and moving on. They fluffed her hair and picked at her clothes until you wanted to slap her hands into stillness.

"I appreciate your coming to see me, really, really appreciate it."

She was bird-bone thin, her chest sunken and collarbones jutting out from under the polyester blouse she wore. She looked as though even the gentlest of touches could break her. Her skin was pale and her hair was an orange color with white roots. With no makeup on, she looked tired and washed out.

Her hands, close to her chest, went round and round each other. "So many people forget you when you've been away for a while."

Her words made me feel like a fraud.

"I just can't get used to the idea that Holly is gone." She started to cry in a soft, unobtrusive way, tears spilling silently down her cheeks. "Poor Holly."

Aunt Kay rose and moved her chair over to sit beside Mrs. Mitchell. The two women, sitting side by side, looked like a before and after picture of extreme weight loss.

Cradling Mrs. Mitchell against her, Aunt Kay made all the soothing sounds necessary.

I looked away.

Mrs. Mitchell started to talk about Holly. Her account was long and rambling, with lots of details about people I'd never heard of, just the way Holly told a story.

This is what it came down to. Three years before, the Mitchells moved up to Georgia for an amazing job opportunity. In Atlanta, Mr. Mitchell met someone else and stayed there with all their worldly possessions. About April Marnie Mitchell had returned to Florida and this sad little apartment at the end of the runway.

"Starting over is so hard, especially when you're alone," Mrs. Mitchell said.

Aunt Kay said, "But at least Holly was near."

Mrs. Mitchell shook her head. "I never saw her. She always promised but something always came up."

"I really had it in my mind that Holly had a baby," Aunt Kay said.

"No, sweetie," Mrs. Mitchell patted Aunt Kay's hand. "You must be mixing her up with someone else. Holly never got a chance to do all that. She wanted to be in show business, to be famous, so you see she couldn't have a baby. She was waiting to have a family until after she had her career. Now I'll never be a grandma." Her tears started again, and I wished I'd waited outside. They didn't really need me and it would have been about the same temperature. The air conditioner was working about as well as the drooping screens on the porch.

Aunt Kay asked, "When are you having a service for Holly?"

"As soon as her body is released, her father will come down." Her right hand went to her hair and wavered over the crown. "I must get my hair done. We'll have a memorial service when he gets here, or more a celebration of her life. I think that's how it should be, don't you?"

A plane took off over our heads and we all looked up. When we could hear ourselves speak again, Aunt Kay said, "Yes, of course. And I'd like to help. If you could give me a list of her closest friends in high school I'll get in touch with them and advise them of the memorial service."

"Oh, that's so sweet of you." Mrs. Mitchell shed more tears.

Aunt Kay stood up and turned her chair back to the two-person dining table. "Let's make out the list now, while I'm here, and I can begin."

She pulled out the second chair before settling herself down at the table. "I'm sure you'll think of more people over the next few days, and I can always call them as well, but this will give me a good start."

It took the better part of another hour and several glasses of ice tea to get out of there. Aunt Kay handed me the list as I unlocked the passenger door. There were only three names on it. Unfortunately, there were no phone numbers to go with them.

I handed the list back to Aunt Kay and helped her into the pickup. "Maybe she didn't know any of Holly's friends."

"Do you know any of these girls?" Aunt Kay asked.

"Yes. Lisa is a flight attendant and lives up north. She came into the Sunset with some friends one night when Holly was working. They sat at the bar, having a high old time, and Holly kept drifting by to talk to them. It was really ticking me off—she had tables to wait. Holly finally got down to business after Lisa told her that she didn't have what it took to be any kind of an actress or model; told Holly she wasn't tall enough or pretty enough."

Aunt Kay gave a little hiss of annoyance. "No wonder you remember her."

"I sure hope that isn't where Angel is. But I don't think Holly would consider Lisa the kind of friend you give a baby to, and really, how old is Lisa? Holly's age, twenty-one, twenty-two at most, too young to take on a child not her own. I don't know the other people on the list . . . Amber? Is that her name?"

Aunt Kay nodded.

"Well, would anyone Holly's age be prepared to raise someone else's child?"

"You have a point. But maybe there is someone who knew, someone who would have a reason to take Angel."

"Who?"

"Dan has a sister a few years older than him. She'd have a reason to take her brother's baby."

"Without telling Dan?"

"Maybe Holly contacted her and told her about the affair with Dan. If Dee wanted to avoid a family confrontation, she would adopt Angel without telling anyone Dan was Angel's father."

"I hope it's true. It would be the best solution for Angel."

"I'll call Dan's mother about the memorial. Grandchildren will come up naturally when I ask about Dee. Did you find a yearbook, some way of tracking down people Holly knew?"

"No, and it wouldn't help us unless we close our eyes and stick a pin in a picture."

CHAPTER 31

It was the quiet period in the bar, before people sneak away from work and a little too early for the regulars to stop in on their way home.

I was alone, slicing up lemons and filling up the trays of garnishes, with Tom Waits growling in the background. This was my time of the day, doing routine tasks, getting ready for the evening to come, settling into myself and thinking about nothing. I like this time. That was only one of the reasons I groaned when Cal Vachess walked in.

He grinned at me like he was sure I was glad to see him. I've been a bartender so long no one would ever know I wasn't happy when they appeared.

No longer concerned with impressing me, Cal clambered up on the bar chair by holding onto the back of the seat and stepping up on a rung, swiveling around and settling down. He got a good look at my leopard print and leather and said, "You didn't have to get all dolled up for me, but I like it."

"Did they run out of booze in Sarasota?"

"It's the bartender, not the booze, I'm interested in."

And that's what was worrying me. I set a Jim Beam in front of him. The conversation went around in circles for a bit and then he got to what I figured had brought him. "So . . . you find Holly's little girl yet?"

"Nope, and we're not going to either. Aunt Kay was just upset by Holly's death and needed to feel she was doing something."

I looked up from the glasses I was unloading from a tray. "Why are you taking such a big interest in Holly's baby? I thought you barely knew Holly."

"Maybe it's not Holly I'm interested in. Maybe she's just an excuse to see you." He leered.

I tossed the towel over my shoulders. "Oh, please, don't try that one on me. You don't have the chops for it. It's Holly you're interested in all right."

He grimaced and said, "Actually, it's her baby. I thought there might be a little money to be had in this situation. People might pay to know where the baby ended up."

"Well, good luck to you if you find the baby and then find someone who cares. I don't think anyone but Aunt Kay is interested in the kid and she hasn't any money." I considered him a bit before I added, "I think you may have another reason for finding the baby."

"Oh, yeah? What's that?"

"You want to know if your brother is the father."

"Why would I think that?"

"Because you know your brother dated Holly months ago and your brother is reckless and stupid."

He raised his palms and his shoulders. "Okay, you got me. I thought it might be Ryan's baby. That thing with Holly went on a long time before I knew anything about it."

When lying becomes an Olympic event, I'll be representing the US . . . a gold medal winner for sure, but I got to thinking right there and then that Cal might be on the podium next to me.

"Why don't you just ask Ryan if he's the father?"

"He never tells a straight story, and if the baby is his, well . . ."

He drew the word out and shrugged his shoulders. "We take care of our own."

"You would take the baby?"

"Sure." He made it sound like I was crazy for thinking anything else. "Actually, I been working it out in my mind. You know, what it would be like to have a kid around, growing up and going to school, all those things." He looked sheepish. "It wouldn't be so bad."

I turned away to hide my face from him. A man who lived off women, proposing to raise a little girl? I had a vision of Uncle Cal interrupting a bedtime story to take a call from a john, saying, "Sorry, honey, Uncle Cal just has to find a nice lady for this man to screw."

"I'd get someone to live in and take care of her but I'd be there until after lunch. I could do that much. I work mostly at night, but I could even work from home if I needed to."

The thought creeped me out and turned me crazy.

"If the baby is Ryan's, I want it."

And if she wasn't Ryan's, Cal might still want her. Maybe I hadn't been too excited about this baby search in the beginning, maybe it was all about the money for me, but the horror of the Vachess brothers with a child was a game changer. No way was Cal Vachess getting anywhere near Angel if I could help it.

"A little girl," he grinned. "It would be nice to have a little girl around."

A chill went down my spine. What was to stop him from selling a child as well as adults? "It isn't Ryan's baby." My voice was too loud in the empty room.

"How do you know?"

"The father is in the army, that's what Holly said. She told Aunt Kay all about Denny."

His glass thunked down on the bar. It only took him a minute to choose how he was going to handle this news. "I'll decide when I see the baby if it's Ryan's."

·"The baby was born before Holly met Ryan. Doesn't matter anyway. The baby is dead."

"What?"

"It's so sad. Don't tell Aunt Kay. I'm trying to keep it from her."

"You sure?" His stare turned me to ice.

I nodded. "It's too much for Aunt Kay to hear after Holly's suicide. I don't know how to tell her. I just told her I'd try to find the baby to ease her mind a little."

His eyes narrowed.

I gave it my all. "I can understand why Holly took her life. First the guy leaves her, and then her little baby dies. Holly was never what you could call a strong person."

He stared at me intently. He hadn't made up his mind yet if he believed me.

"It was some birth defect." I patted my chest. "Her heart, something called Wolff-Parkinson-White syndrome, that's why she died."

Maybe it was the words *birth defect*, or the impressive reality of the name, but he winced as if I'd slapped him. Cal believed me now.

He looked away. "A little girl. I . . . well, I was making plans."

He gave a small bitter laugh and his eyes came back to me. "I was even planning to redo a room and went to one of those kid's places to look at furniture. It was going to be all pink and frilly with a white crib . . . lots of stupid ideas."

He picked up his glass, started to take a drink but set it down on the wood instead, missing the napkin. He pushed the glass around and watched as the damp circles grew. "I thought maybe . . . I thought she might be like me."

His jaw turned to granite. He put the palms of his hands flat on the bar and thrust his prominent chin towards me as if he expected me to argue. "Well, those silly ideas will stop now." It was as if I'd tricked him into having such thoughts and he was angry at me for suggesting it.

"Sorry," I said. What was I apologizing for? But it seemed to be necessary. "I'm surprised you thought Holly's baby was Ryan's. Didn't you ask him how long he'd known Holly?"

"Ryan just says what makes things easiest for him and what he thinks I want to hear. I thought I'd take a look at the kid."

I laughed now, as much in relief as anything. "Did you think you could tell by looking at a baby that it was Ryan's?"

He gave me a sheepish smile. "Kinda dumb, huh?"

"Kinda." But maybe he just wanted it to be true, wanted her to be Ryan's, needed to have someone else to live for when Ryan's excesses killed him.

Or maybe Cal had other weird plans that I didn't want to think about.

I left the restaurant just after eleven, earlier than most nights, and ahead of Miguel. Whatever was behind Cal's search for Angel, I believed my lies meant I was done with the Vachess brothers. I thought I was safe.

Still, I made sure I left the building with a group of diners, walked quickly to my truck under the light by the door, had my keys sticking out through my fingers in a defensive mode and locked the door behind me as soon as I was safely inside.

For all my precautions I felt more cheerful and secure than I had in months. But like always I watched for lights in the rearview on the drive out the beach. I had the road all to myself. I turned on the radio, listening to my favorite Tampa rock station and relaxing, going home and thinking about cashing Aunt Kay's check, planning who I'd pay and who I'd let slide a bit. It gave me a sense of power over the people who had been dunning me for money. A minor win but I'd take it.

All in all I was pleased with myself. I'd kept Aunt Kay happy and got rid of Cal Vachess. And if I never found Angel it didn't matter; I figured I'd stopped Cal from looking for her. I felt good about that.

It was garbage pickup the next morning. Taking out the trash constitutes housekeeping for me. In the kitchen, I dumped my keys and purse on a chair and kicked off the red stilettos. I pulled the bag out of the can below the sink and slipped on my flip-flops.

In the darkness of the carport, while I tied a knot in the handles of the plastic grocery bag, I listened to crash of the waves and small critters chirping and croaking in the thick underbrush, a secret chorus in the night.

I wheeled the trash can out towards the road, the warm night air on my skin and the smell of saltwater soothing me as the large rubber container rumbled over the sand and crushed shells of the drive.

Suddenly a light appeared at the end of the drive. Without thinking, I let go of the bin and darted into the sea grapes growing along the driveway. The crackle of the deep leaves under my feet seemed too loud. The smell of sandalwood rose around me and suddenly the night was silent.

I craned my neck to look down the drive and watched the light dance. It was the same light I'd seen the night before. Then the overhead came on in the car and I saw clearly inside the vehicle parked across the end of the drive.

Cal Vachess was talking on his cell. He looked down at something on the seat beside him as he talked on the phone. Then he slapped his cell together and reached up and turned off the overhead. It was black again.

CHAPTER 32

My heart revved into overdrive, adrenaline making me light-headed. Frozen there in indecision, I was afraid if I broke cover and ran up the drive for the house he'd see me, but I was scared that if I stayed where I was, he might come up the driveway, see the trash can and know I was there. Either way I wasn't safe—so did I run for the house or push through jungle to the neighbors? There was no going back if I made the wrong choice.

I wanted my phone but the house would be the first place Cal looked for me. And even if I dialed 911, how long would it be before help came? But the gun was in the nightstand. That was more important than the phone.

And what if he wasn't alone?

The undergrowth was thick. Branches gouged my leather skirt and snagged my top as I burrowed deeper and deeper into their midst, pushing my way through the underbrush and hoping the noise wouldn't reach the road.

I felt blood trickling down my arm. It didn't matter. I stopped to listen to the night that had suddenly gone still. Then I began again, telling myself to go silently, slowly picking my way through the forest of vegetation so I didn't give away my position, easing through the jungle in case there was another car parked in the drive next door. I didn't want to run smack into a second watcher, wanted to see them before they saw me.

I came out in the sea grapes lining my neighbor's driveway. No lights shone from the house. The owners hadn't arrived yet for the season and the tradesmen had gone home. The lane was empty. I was alone.

I listened and waited as the night came alive once more. Small insects clicked and tree toads chirped, but there were no human sounds, no sound of traffic or car doors slamming, no sounds of Cal getting out of the truck, of his cowboy boots crunching up the drive.

But why would he do that? He had me cornered. Who or what was he waiting for? Ryan Vachess was the only answer.

I made myself smaller while my terrified mind churned over the possibilities of what the Vachess brothers wanted with me. Maybe Cal hadn't believed my story about the dead baby and thought I had Angel. If he meant to steal a baby he wasn't planning on leaving witnesses. And even worse than dying was the thought of what Ryan Vachess would do to me before he killed me.

Deep in my belly a keening hum of fear rose to my lips. I covered my mouth to silence it while my fevered brain ran up and down the corridors of possible escape . . . of help. There was no help for me.

Waiting was harder than running. Did I go towards the beach or to the road? I slipped off my shoes and bent over at the waist to form a smaller shadow, creeping slowly down the edge of the blackness from the scrub. I needed to see what was happening at the road.

There was only one vehicle parked across the driveway. I hunkered down and watched as Cal took calls and made calls. It seemed to be business as usual, until the final call. The light from his cell went out and the engine came on. I could hear gravel spinning out from his tires as he sped away.

Would he be back? I stayed crouched down in the shadows until some small thing ran over my foot. I was gone; sprinting faster than my heart was beating, flying towards the beach. Kicking up sand behind me, I dove down over the edge of a sand dune on my stomach. Somewhere along the way I'd lost both of my flip-flops. Getting to my knees, I crawled to the top of the bank and searched the darkness. My well-lit house stood out like a beacon.

I lifted my head further to see if my footprints showed, but it was too dark to distinguish anything in the sand. Unless someone who was hunting me had a flashlight, I was safe where I was. I crouched down again. But did I want to stay here? I had to decide.

I had two other choices—run up the beach to find a house that was occupied or risk driving away from the beach. Taking the truck meant I had to go back inside the house to get my keys.

If Cal was coming back there might not be much time. I had to make up my mind.

I lifted my head and had one more look about and then I bolted for the house. Inside in seconds, I grabbed my purse and keys and ran into the bedroom to get Clay's gun.

I didn't stop to lock the doors before running for the truck.

Accelerating backwards, I hit the trash can, tossing it into the brush, and rocketed out onto the road without slowing. Driving in the dark without lights, barely able to see the road, I hoped if I met Cal coming back to the house he wouldn't recognize my red pickup until I flashed by.

When I reached the south bridge I turned on my lights and headed off island. I called Brian.

CHAPTER 33

In the morning I awoke to a new terrifying reality. How many days ago had I only been worried about saving the Sunset? Now it was my own survival that was on the top of my worry list.

I thought I'd gotten rid of Cal Vachess when I told him Angel was dead but it hadn't stopped him from coming after me. If he wasn't hunting for the baby, what was he after? He'd sat at the end of the drive for two nights in a row. Why?

"Do you want to go to the police?" Brian asked.

"Oh yeah, that always works well, doesn't it? They only arrest people after the fact, not for what they might do."

"Then call Clay and tell him to come home."

If I called Clay and asked him to come home, it would look like a ploy to get him away from Laura. I didn't want him on those terms. Clay had to come back to me because he wanted to.

"Clay already thinks I'm crazy; let's not make it worse."

But Brian was only worried about the immediate problem of Cal Vachess.

My leather skirt and leopard top were ruined so Brian drove me back out to the beach house for clothes. We coasted by my rent-free house. It no longer seemed like the deal of a lifetime. Brian pulled into the next driveway, where I'd hidden in the underbrush. It was a melee of activity with people coming and going, carrying boards, tools and buckets in their hands.

Brian turned around and drifted back to the entrance to the laneway. "What do you think?"

"No car, and with all these people next door, I think it's safe."

"Okay." He pulled slowly in and crept towards the beach. "We'll pull up to the house and have a good look before we decide if we go in."

"What if they left someone inside?" My voice cracked.

"I'll check it out. You wait in the car until I tell you to come in. Okay?"

"Sure."

When he got out of the car, I locked the door and slipped behind the wheel. My right hand was on the revolver in my purse.

Even when he stood at the door to the kitchen and waved to me, it took a few minutes for me to unlock the car door and join him in the house.

Inside, I went to the bedroom and quickly started packing a bag. The first thing that went into my suitcase was the whole box of ammunition. Then I added clothes.

"I had a visitor," I said as soon as Aunt Kay opened her back door to me and before she could tell me I was late. "After work, about midnight, when I was out at the beach house alone."

"Who?"

"Cal Vachess."

Her eyes opened wider. She went around me to the door and latched the chain and then she asked, "What did he want?"

"I don't know." I pulled a chair out from the table and dumped my purse onto it. "I want to know how he found me. My address isn't listed anywhere. Most of my staff don't know where I live. It's safer that way. He probably followed me home Monday night. But why? Why is he watching me?"

"I can't begin to guess." She opened the fridge and sat a sweating jug of ice tea on the table.

"After last night I thought I'd convinced him to forget about me." I ran my hands through my hair and paced. "I told him Angel was dead."

A glass shattered on the floor.

"Oh, sorry, not really. Cal came into the Sunset last night and I lied about Angel being dead, hoping he'd back off."

She looked uncertain, like she was trying to judge if I was telling her the truth.

I raised my right hand and said, "I know nothing about Angel that you don't know."

She nodded, believing me now. "Okay."

She bent over and got out a small brush and a tray hanging beneath the sink. I took them from her trembling hands and swept up the shattered glass while she sank down onto a chair.

"How do we stop this . . . this stalking you?"

"I don't know. I thought I ended it last night in the Sunset but it looks like he's still searching for Angel."

"What have I started? Do you want me to phone Cal Vachess and say we aren't interested in Holly or her baby anymore?"

"Now that would be subtle, wouldn't it? I already told him that Holly's baby is dead. If he doesn't believe that, he won't believe anything else we say."

"It might keep him away from you." She braced herself on the table and leaned forward. "Unless it isn't the baby he's interested in." Her face got real worried. "Maybe it isn't about Angel." Her face was constricted with fear. "Oh, Sherri, you don't think he has a crush on you, do you?"

"If a crush is something sexual, I can pretty much guarantee that he doesn't have physical designs on me."

Her body softened. "Then it has something to do with Holly, but what?"

Did I really want to tell her what I'd come up with? One way or another, if it was true she had to know. "Maybe the Vachess brothers already have the baby."

She gave a little gasp of shock and covered her mouth with her hand. I poured a glass of tea and pushed it towards her.

She took a sip and then said, "Why would they be following you if that was true?"

"Maybe they don't want us stirring up trouble."

Aunt Kay said, "What a mess. It seemed so simple." With her elbow on the table, she rubbed her forehead. "It doesn't make any sense. I can almost believe he was interested in the baby because it might be Ryan's, and maybe Cal even thought that the baby would be born with his condition. It would be understandable that he might feel close to the child under those circumstances, but if he believes the baby is dead, or if he already has the baby, why is he still hanging around your house? And why would he draw attention to himself by coming into the Sunset if he has Angel?"

I had no answer to her questions.

And then a look of total shock came over her face. "What if he didn't believe Angel was dead and thinks you have her?"

I blew out a deep breath and said, "We're only guessing. It could be any one of these or none. What do you want to do now?"

"We don't need to go near the Vachess brothers, but I still want to look for Angel." Her eyes were fixed on my face. "Are you okay with that?"

I'd already stepped in the hornet's nest and dropping the hunt for Angel wouldn't change that. The bottom line was I needed the money, but there was another reason I wasn't quitting. "I want to find Angel. No one but us cares about her and there's no goddamn way I'm letting perverts like the Vachess brothers have her."

"Good." She gave a determined nod. "But we have to hurry."

"Yes, we need to find her before Cal does."

"I wasn't actually thinking of that. I go into the hospital Sunday."

"Are you sure you want to go on asking about the baby if you're about to have this surgery?"

She smiled. "The phrase *now or never* has never been more apt."

"Shouldn't you be resting?"

"And worrying? No thank you. I want to find Angel. "

"Okay, but there is one thing more bothering me."

She had started to push herself up from the table. She stopped and waited.

"What if the baby is already with the Vachess brothers, what do we do then?"

She took a deep breath and pushed herself upright. "I guess we'll answer that question when we come to it."

She went to the counter and pulled a wicker basket towards her, took out a checkbook and started writing. She came back to the table and laid the check down in front of me.

It was dated that day and was in the full amount. "You deserve it," she said.

I pulled out the original check she'd written and handed it over to her. While she ripped it up, I tucked the new check away, glad to have it but knowing that the search had gone far past my need to pay the mortgage. I was going on even if Aunt Kay decided to stop.

And if I couldn't find Angel I had another plan. If all else failed I intended to blackmail and bully Dan into taking over the search for his baby. There was no way I was letting him walk away from this— no way was I leaving Angel out there alone.

CHAPTER 34

Aunt Kay's phone rang. She raised an eyebrow at me.

"Might be your doctor." But still I braced myself for more evil from the Vachess brothers.

She nodded and went to the phone. After saying hello, she gave me the thumbs up and said, "Yes, Marnie." She listened some more. "Yes of course. Sherri is with me now." A huge smile spread across Aunt Kay's face. "We'll come right over, if that's convenient, and then we can go up to Sarasota and get Holly's things."

She ended the call and said, "The police are all finished in Holly's apartment. It seems the owner wants the unit back and Marnie Mitchell wants me to go up to Sarasota with her to collect Holly's belongings. Marnie doesn't have a car."

"Were you the only person Mrs. Mitchell could think to call?"

"It appears so." Aunt Kay tilted her head a little and said, "I wonder how we can go through Holly's possessions without upsetting her?"

It didn't take her long to think of something. "After we check out the apartment and load Holly's stuff in the truck, I'll offer to buy Marnie lunch. You say you have a few errands to run. While we're having lunch, you drive somewhere out of sight and go through everything to see what you can find. I'm sure there has to be something in Holly's belongings that will tell us where Angel is."

"You aren't the nice lady I thought you were."

"Sorry about that." She picked up a white visor and her wrap-around sunglasses. She was ready to go.

Marnie Mitchell was waiting outside for us. When we stopped in front of her she came to the truck and opened the crew door before I could get out. Once inside the truck she said, "Thank you."

Aunt Kay turned to Mrs. Mitchell and smiled warmly. "We're delighted to help."

"You were so kind to me, coming to see me and all, you were the first ones I thought of when the police phoned. There was no one else really. Thank you."

Aunt Kay said, "It will be easier when Holly's father is here to share the burden with you."

"He can't come down."

Aunt Kay and I exchanged looks.

"He said he can't get away."

Glancing in the rearview I saw her tears start.

"And he said it wouldn't do any good anyway. He's going to send me half of the cost of the funeral."

The closer to Sarasota we got, the more she seemed to fold into herself, appearing smaller and smaller each time I checked in the mirror.

This time the super opened the door for us. Up close she had olive skin and a faint mustache but she seemed friendlier than she had before. I'd worried all the way to Sarasota how awkward it might be if she mentioned that we were there before, but Bella only said, "Sorry for your loss," and led the way to the elevator, pushing a luggage cart.

Truthfully, Mrs. Mitchell wouldn't have noticed if Bella had said a hundred people had come by asking about Holly.

Bella opened the door to the apartment and stepped aside. "I'll wait here, give you some privacy."

"Thank you." Pushing the luggage trolley, I led the way with it into the apartment.

Aunt Kay practically had to drag Mrs. Mitchell inside. She hovered near the door, looking like she might bolt at any second. Her eyes grew wide with surprise and darted around the room. "I don't understand."

Aunt Kay wrapped her arms around Mrs. Mitchell's shoulders and began making soothing noises.

Starkly modern, the apartment was done in tones of white, cream and beige, with glass and steel furniture sitting on plush carpeting and ebony hardwood. Dan had said that everything was packed and the apartment was neat. He hadn't exaggerated. Against the wall by the entrance was a small pile of things. Other than that, the room was bare of any sign of human life, not a potted plant nor a discarded magazine in sight.

I went to check out the rest of the rooms.

In the bedroom there was a wall of mirrored closets where not even dust had been left behind. Across from the closets the sheer curtains were open on the million-dollar view over Sarasota Bay.

I turned away and opened the bedside table. Not even lint. Who leaves a place this clean?

In the bathroom fresh towels awaited new arrivals, just like in a hotel.

My search didn't take long. The person who packed up hadn't left any traces of the woman named Holly Mitchell except for the small pile of belongings near the front door.

On the way back to the living room, I went into the galley kitchen. It was so clean it looked like not even water had been boiled in there and it smelled of antiseptic cleaner. The first thing I did was open the doors of the refrigerator, maybe because that's what I always do when I enter my own kitchen. The fridge was empty, not even half a jar of mayo left behind. Okay, say that Holly was obsessive about neatness and cleanliness; even so, does anyone move out and leave a place this bare?

At the edge of the door, between the wall and the fridge, I saw a sharp corner of a piece of paper, just a tiny triangle no more than a quarter of an inch. I closed the fridge and could no longer see it. I opened the door again and tried to reach the paper with my fingers, but they wouldn't fit. I took two steak knives from a wooden block on the counter and, using them like tweezers, I locked onto a curled corner and pulled the sheet forward to where I could reach it with the door closed. The paper was dry and crumpled from life behind the fridge.

I studied the grainy image, printed by an ordinary desk-jet printer, of a woman holding a baby. Then I carefully folded the sheet and stuck it in my purse.

In the living room Mrs. Mitchell had refused to budge from her position by the entrance. "I can't," she said when Aunt Kay asked her once again if she didn't want to look in the other rooms. She'd already seen too much. Her cocoon of ignorance had been destroyed and her memories tainted.

"There's nothing left in there anyway," I told them. "I looked everywhere, checked all the drawers and cupboards."

Mrs. Mitchell's soft response was, "It doesn't matter." Her voice was full of defeat. Nothing was going to matter to her for a long time.

I pushed the luggage cart closer to the pile of boxes and started loading. There were two large wheeled suitcases, a cardboard box full of beauty products and two lidded plastic bins full of photo albums. There were also three more plastic bins full of shoes and purses. Still, it wasn't a lot for twenty-one years of life.

Bella waited in the hall to lock the door.

"Did you clean the apartment?" I asked.

She looked like I was accusing her of a crime. "The property manager called and told me to go through it after the police left. Everything personal I found I added to those bins, only a few things, and then I gave it a good cleaning just like I was told."

"Bella, who owns the apartment?"

Her eyes slid sideways to Mrs. Mitchell. "You'll have to ask the property manager about that." She took hold of the luggage cart and pushed it towards the elevator.

CHAPTER 35

After leaving the Jade Towers apartments I dropped Aunt Kay and Mrs. Mitchell off at the first family restaurant we saw. Mrs. Mitchell looked like she didn't care if she ever ate again, but she didn't protest when Aunt Kay led her away.

Around the corner from the restaurant I pulled in behind an office building and climbed into the truck bed, trying to decide where to start. The bins were easiest so I began checking in every purse for stray papers, old tissues, receipts or notes. That was the strangest thing. Every purse was perfectly empty. Not even some leftover coins. This wasn't Bella's work. Was it Holly who'd emptied them all out? The featherhead Holly I knew wasn't that obsessive. Maybe someone just opened every purse and dumped the contents into a garbage bag.

The tubs full of photos took the most time because I got caught up in watching Holly morph through years and through styles. The camera adored Holly and gave her a unique allure that the living, breathing Holly didn't have. The studio shots Ryan Vachess took were the very best of the whole collection, more art than reality, showing a vulnerable woman with a haunting fragility, the bubbling, enthusiastic Holly gone astray. And something more, a transitory loveliness, like a flower that only blooms for a day. There were no photos like the ones on the Angel Escort website, just page after page of her beauty.

Why hadn't she made it in the world of modeling? With her willingness to please and the way the camera captured her beauty, she should have made it to the top. Maybe Holly was right and she just never got the right break.

In the last container of publicity stills and promotional shots I found a silver picture frame. When I turned it over I was staring at myself and Holly posing on a beach. I was captured in the act of drying off my left leg, half bent over and looking up at the person taking the picture and with all my charms about to tumble out of my bikini top.

I would have sworn I'd never been on a beach with Holly but the table in the background brought back the memory of mimosas and French pastries. The sister of one of the bartenders at the Sunset had organized a birthday brunch on the beach one Sunday morning in early summer. We'd only been there for about two hours. By noon, walking on the sand was like walking on fire.

Holly hadn't framed and kept the picture because of me but because she'd been unable to cut me out and still keep the terrific photograph of her. It was from her blonde bombshell phase. In the photo she was standing on her toes, wearing a bikini and holding a towel, leaning forward from the waist and doing sort of a Madonna imitation. It was a sizzling print. It really, really worked and explained why Ryan thought he knew me. For a minute I thought of keeping it for myself. What would it hurt?

I turned it upside down and set it back in the box and took out a small plastic album, cheap but new-looking, the kind you can buy in any drugstore. My fingers stuck to the plastic with sweat as I turned the pages of baby pictures of a child in the first weeks of life. Holly wasn't in any of the pictures. Maybe she was behind the camera. I took out each one of them and checked the back but they told me nothing more.

I stared at the pictures, trying to see Holly or Dan or signs of anyone else. Was this the child Shelly had handed to me, was this Hannah? I couldn't tell. For me it was just a formless little being. There were no secrets there for me to discover.

Mrs. Mitchell wouldn't understand why Holly had the pictures of a baby. Should I keep the album out or put it back, leave them there to raise questions, or take them out and deprive her of the only contact she'd have with her granddaughter? In the end I put the tiny book back in the bin.

The oversized, wheeled suitcases contained expensive clothes in pristine condition. There was nothing that you'd do housework in or wear to paint a bathroom. There wasn't even a pair of shabby pajamas for when she got sick. It was like every inch of her life was glamorous.

I sat back on my heels and considered the pile. Holly's past was missing. There was no life before she went to live in that white apartment and nothing to give us a clue to Holly's friends. Where were all her other belongings? It was unlikely that Holly had left them behind with Mrs. Mitchell. Maybe Holly's past went into a garbage bag as well.

There was no phone and no computer in the bins, but the police might have those. I did find a small pink-leather address book with phone numbers and addresses of modeling agencies and other professional contacts. I looked under *T*, but my name wasn't there. Neither was Aunt Kay's. Neither was the phone number of the Sunset. I flipped through the book to see if any name jumped out at me or if a name looked like it didn't fit. Nothing.

In a zippered plastic pouch I found her bank statements and a checkbook that showed she had two hundred dollars in the bank. There were no keys, wallet, social security card, none of that. In the end, my search raised more questions than it answered.

CHAPTER 36

I unloaded the last bin into Marnie Mitchell's living room where Holly's possessions took up most of the empty floor space. The temperature inside the tiny west-facing box was barely cooler than outside, probably well into the nineties, but Mrs. Mitchell was unaware of the heat. She sat on a straight-back chair, her arms wrapped tightly across her chest, and rocked back and forth, staring at the leftovers of her daughter's life that I had stacked in front of her. Finally, when the last bin had been added to the pile, she said, "The police told me who paid for that apartment."

Aunt Kay pulled up a chair and sat beside her. "Why don't you tell me? You'll feel better sharing."

Mrs. Mitchell shook her head. "Nothing will make me feel better." She looked from the pile of her daughter's belongings to Aunt Kay. "When I heard his name I was proud at first, but only at first . . . until I realized . . ." She lowered her gaze to her lap and said, ". . . what it meant."

Mrs. Mitchell went back to staring at the heap of containers. "You know him, you must know him. We all did." The name was barely whispered. "Dusty Harrison."

Aunt Kay showed surprise. She looked to me but I just shrugged my shoulders. The name meant nothing.

"You mean the singer?" Aunt Kay asked.

"Yes." Mrs. Mitchell started to hum and I recognized a silly

Christmas song that you hear in every mall all December long. Mrs. Mitchell said, "He wrote that, you know."

"I didn't realize," Aunt Kay said.

"Oh, yes. He wrote all his own material. I used to have some of his albums, loved his voice." Mrs. Mitchell hummed another song.

I knew this sappy love song. "You mean the singer my mother used to listen to and go weak at the knees over, that's Dusty Harrison?"

"Yes," Mrs. Mitchell said. "That's him, a real talent."

Aunt Kay, with her hands planted on her widespread knees, swiveled her body to look at me. "He was a big star thirty years ago. He still sings at every charity event in Southwest Florida."

Mrs. Mitchell nodded. "A living legend, that's what they call him."

"And the apartment?" Aunt Kay asked. "Was he paying for the apartment?"

"The police said he owned it."

"And he let Holly live there?"

Mrs. Mitchell pinched her lips together in a thin line like she was trying to stop words from bursting out.

Aunt Kay reached out and took her hand. "Did the police talk to him?"

"I don't know; don't know anything more about it."

I closed the door as gently as possible behind us. "Is she going to be all right?"

Aunt Kay gave a small lift of her shoulders. "How do you survive the death of a child, never mind that she's only coming to realize some unpleasant things about her daughter? It will take a while for her to smooth over events and create a story she can live with."

I took Aunt Kay's elbow as she stepped stiffly down the steps and onto the path.

When she had both feet firmly on the ground she pulled her arm away from me. "Are you some kind of nurse now?"

"Seems like it."

My tee was sticking to me. "I bet we broke another record for heat today." I pulled the cloth away from my body and fanned it gently. "I'm not going anywhere until I've had a shower and something to eat."

"You really are getting to be a princess." The humidity had her own hair curling up into a tangled halo around her very pale face. This heat wasn't good for her but she wasn't giving in.

"What did you find?" she said when we were back in the truck and she'd stopped panting like a dog.

I pulled the paper out of my purse and had a good look at the baby. "I don't know if this is a picture of Hannah." I handed it to Aunt Kay. "Does it look like the baby Holly brought to show you? Is it Angel?"

"I'm not sure." Aunt Kay pointed to the woman holding the baby. "Who is this woman?"

"I can't tell . . . can't see the face because of the hair."

"Well, I'm sure it isn't Holly." She pulled the photo closer to her face. "The baby is Angel. I'm sure of it." She lowered the printout. "Were there more pictures of Angel?"

"There was a small baby album but nothing to say who the photos were of or where they were taken. It looked like Angel's first month of life, but no pictures of Holly in any of them. I left the album there."

"I'm surprised there weren't later pictures of Angel."

"Maybe there were more pictures on Holly's phone."

"And where is that?"

"I don't know. Dan said he checked her messages, so it was there when her body was discovered. Maybe he took the phone because his number was on it."

"Will you call him and find out?"

"I'm not really happy doing that."

"Well, I'm not paying you to be happy, am I?" Aunt Kay went back to studying the printout as though she could discover some hidden truth. She kept at it all the way back to her house.

CHAPTER 37

When I came out of her bathroom, Aunt Kay greeted me with, "Cal Vachess is outside."

Her news made my stomach turn over. "How do you know?" I moved to stand beside her at the window.

"Please, a black Cadillac Escalade on this street stands out like a biker in Sunday School."

She held out a pair of old-fashioned field glasses. "Besides, I got out my binoculars and had a closer look."

"Why would he be watching your house?" I took the glasses from her hand and stared at the suv parked on the opposite side of the street. "It's him all right."

"I bet he knows you're here. Your truck in the drive is a dead giveaway."

"How did he find out where you live?"

"I left my phone number when I called him. Could he find out from that?"

I lowered the glasses. "What the hell does he want with me?"

She took back the glasses. "What do you want to do?"

Across the street a man mowed his lawn. Next door, two kids ran through a sprinkler while their mother watched from the front step. Whatever was on Cal's mind he wasn't going to act on it in broad daylight with all these people as witnesses. "I'm going to get in my truck and go to the Sunset."

"Are you sure?" Aunt Kay's voice was full of doubt.

"I'm sure. It's me he wants, not you. Don't worry."

"I'm not concerned about me. What if he follows you?"

"He knows where I work so he doesn't need to follow me. He can pick me up anytime." I had a horrible thought. "If he's looking for the baby and he thinks you might know something, he might come in here and threaten you."

"I won't answer the door."

"That might not be enough."

"Hear those kids screaming next door?" She pointed at the kids in the sprinkler. "Their dad is a policeman and he'll be home anytime now. I'll call him if Cal gets out of his vehicle. Just you be careful and phone me when you get to the Sunset."

I made two calls and then I left, not even looking over to where Cal waited, but I watched as he followed me over the bridge across the inland waters and out the beach to the Sunset.

At the Sunset Cal pulled into the lot and then swung around to face the street. I couldn't figure out why he was stopping out there.

I parked by the alley that ran behind the building. Miguel stood at the bottom of the stairs to the kitchen door. He was carrying a meat cleaver, what Miguel likes to call his attitude adjuster, Mexican-style. A few guys had quickly changed their attitude when Miguel came out of the kitchen with his chopper. Except for the cleaver hanging from his hand, Miguel looked like he'd just stepped out to enjoy a cigarette before the evening rush started.

He dropped the cigarette, wiggled his toe on the butt, and then came to the truck as I opened the door. "Where's the guy that's following you?"

"Out front."

"I'll go have a chat with him."

"No. Let's get inside."

I ran up the stairs to safety with Miguel at my back.

The three people working busily in the kitchen, stirring, flipping and frying, barely acknowledged my arrival.

Out front Gwen greeted me with, "The parrots are gone. It was too good to last but it gave us one good day. Oh, and a guy named Ryan Vachess came in looking for you. I told him I wasn't expecting you in tonight. What did you do to piss him off?"

"Not a lot, but sometimes the only way I can't offend people is to stay indoors and not answer the phone." I went past her, heading for the corner window in the long row that overlooked the beach. I looked down on the black Escalade. Was Cal inside the vehicle or was he already in the elevator making his way up to find me?

Gwen said, "We could do with one more server."

"Leave it. The three on duty tonight will be smiling and running their behinds off. They'll be delighted to finally have a full shift." I turned away from the window. "Were there any other calls for me?"

"Some guy called and asked for you. I told him you were with your Aunt Kay but I could take a message. He said no, he knew where your Aunt Kay lived and he'd meet you there."

So that explained how Cal knew where to find me. "Let's not give out any more information." Gwen really hadn't told him anything but still, it bothered me. "Just say you don't know where I am or when I'll be back." I went back to studying Cal's Cadillac.

"Lately, that wouldn't be a lie." Gwen put her hand on my shoulder. "Are you all right?"

"Good question."

"Well, if I can help . . ." She left it at that.

"You always do, Gwennie, you always do."

I was in the office punching in the number for Angel Escort when Tully showed up. I pointed him to a chair and waited for Cal to pick up.

"Angel Escort."

"Cal?"

His "Yeah" was cautious and wary.

"Sherri Travis. Why are you following me?"

"What gave you that dumb idea?"

"You mean you weren't at my house late last night, didn't tail me here from Aunt Kay's and you aren't sitting out in the parking lot at this very moment?"

There was a heavy sigh and then he said, "I'm not stalking you, you stupid bitch, I'm trying to protect you."

It took a minute. "From your brother?"

"Yeah. He's got a big case of the dislikes for you."

"It wouldn't take much, given the chemicals he's ingesting. What exactly is his drug of choice?"

"Meth and a little ecstasy."

And this was the paranoid guy who thought I'd gone looking for him. Not good.

"That's one hell of a combination." My brain was whirring through coping strategies with a guy on a meth cocktail.

Cal said, "Get lost for a few days until I get him sorted out."

"How you gonna do that?"

The silence stretched. At last Cal said, "I'm working on it."

"Work harder." I hit End and dropped the cell on my desk. "Shit."

"Tell me," Tully said.

I filled him in and then said, "Cal's right. I need to get out of here for a few days."

"Let's go see Clay. Do a little fishing. It's been a while since we did that."

"I don't want to leave Aunt Kay. She's going in for surgery and I want to stay close to her until then." I didn't mention that I also wanted to find Angel. Somewhere along the way it had become as important to me as it was to Aunt Kay. "By the time Aunt Kay goes in for her operation Clay will be home." Or not, the spiteful little voice that resides in my head chirped in.

"I'll stay at Brian's and get someone else to work the bar. Everything will be fine."

"Yeah, right." Tully was making for the door. "We'll argue about it later, but for now let's get the hell out of here."

CHAPTER 38

Fleeing the Sunset went off like a textbook FBI operation from the movies. From where Cal was parked near the front entrance, he couldn't see what was happening back of the restaurant. I went out through the kitchen with Miguel, down the alley at the foot of the stairs to where Tully had pulled his beat-up old pickup in beside mine.

I crouched down among the debris on the floor of his truck and Tully threw a plaid shirt, stinking of gasoline, over me. Gwen was on her cell at the window, watching to see that Cal didn't move. I was hoping he'd spend a good long time out there in the parking lot guarding nothing. I pretty much believed him when he said he was trying to protect me from Ryan, but I've been lied to before.

A block away from the Sunset my cell rang. Gwen said, "He's still here."

I slid up onto the seat and checked the rear window to be sure. The street behind us was empty. I was free of the Vachess brothers.

Brian lived in a very upscale development on the north border of the Jacaranda Golf Course, a place where even the help didn't drive vehicles as beat up as Tully's. As we pulled into the brick drive, the door of the garage went up so Tully could pull in beside Brian's Mercedes. The door slid down behind us before the engine was off. We'd all seen too many movies.

Brian's house was on the thirteenth hole of the golf course. Only a long narrow pond separated his lawn from the tee and Brian and I had often practiced chipping from his lawn to the green. But not tonight.

On the lanai with cold drinks in our hands, Brian pointed to the edge of the pond thirty yards away. "That old reptile suns himself there on my property every day."

The gator had to be at least twelve feet long and looked more like a plastic replica than the real thing.

"See," Brian said, gesturing towards a man on the green with a cell phone taking a picture of the gator beside a large white sign that said TRESPASSERS WILL BE VIOLATED. "Someone likes my warning. I've been asked to remove it by both the golf club and by the homeowners' association; seems it lowers the tone of the place."

Tully said, "That big bull is way too large to be around humans."

"Yeah, it's time they got him out of here." Brian leaned forward to put his glass on the coffee table. "The wildlife people are supposed to be coming to remove him this week. Our association has already had four of his size taken out this year."

Tully turned to me. "Don't you go out there until it's gone, Sherri."

"How dumb do you think I am?"

He grinned but refrained from pointing to my current situation as an example. Instead he said, "You've got the best of it all, Brian, a little nature and a great house."

The truth was, Tully hated suburban life even more than I did. He thought golf courses were a blight on the landscape and would normally express this view to anyone who would listen. Either he was really grateful to Brian for taking me in and giving me a spot to hide, or Bernice was teaching Tully to play nice. Oh hell, what was I thinking? Bernice and the word nice didn't belong together.

Brian gave us a small wry smile. "I thought it was a great deal.

Way underpriced when I bought it at the top of the market and in another ten years it may even be worth what I paid for it. I should have learned after the tech bubble, but no, there I was just as excited as all the other clowns to jump back into the latest disaster."

All the regulars at the Sunset had heard about Brian's adventures in investing and took it as an example of how not to make money. "At least you have something to show for it this time."

"Yeah, four empty bedrooms and a pool no one uses." He smiled. "But at least you're here now." He rubbed his hands together. "I'm glad of that, but how much trouble is this guy going to be, Sherri?"

I was feeling like prey, stalked and cornered with the hunter moving in for the kill, but there was no way I was sharing that with Tully and Brian. Their reaction would be extreme and violent. "It will blow over, no worries."

Tully, his brow furrowed in worry lines, asked, "Do you think his brother can control this guy?"

The thing was if Tully heard the wrong answer, he was going to take it upon himself to correct things.

"Sure. In a day or two he'll be all hot and bothered about someone else."

"Better be." Tully leaned forward, elbows on his knees. "If not, I'm going to have a long talk with that boy."

Which was exactly what I was afraid of.

"Do you want me to get a restraining order?" Brian asked.

"You have much more faith in the law than I do. Those things never stop bad things from happening." I tilted my head towards the gator. "You might just as well go out there and wave a piece of paper at that big boy. He'll eat you and the paper."

Brian nodded. "It's true. They only seem to help after the fact."

"Cal will take care of Ryan. I just have to stay out of his line of fire until he loses interest." But I'd rather deal with ten drunks than one guy on meth. "If it's okay with you, I'll stay in your guest room and away from the Sunset for a couple of days."

"Stay as long as you like," Brian said. "I'm happy to have you."

The sound of yapping drew our attention. A small Jack Russell terrier dashed out from the house next door. Darting forward and then stopping to bark, the dog ran to the edge of the pond, startling a heron into the air.

The gator rose from its belly to its legs.

"Dinner," Brian said.

A middle-aged woman ran across the lawn calling, "Benjy, Benjy."

We were all on our feet screaming, "Go back."

The woman hesitated. "Benjy, come here."

She ran forward and scooped the little dog up in her arms. Then she stood there holding the dog and staring at the gator. Even the dog stopped yapping and waited for the attack.

The gator paused and then turned and slid into the water.

We all took deep breaths and began talking at once.

"Stupid woman," Brian said and headed for the door. "I'm going over to talk to her."

Tully slumped into a chair.

"I have to go make some calls," I said, the first call being to Marley to make sure she didn't go near the beach house. Even though the dental office was closed for the week, and she was out at the ranch and wasn't supposed to come into Jacaranda, I didn't want her to pop into town for lunch and accidently bump into either of the Vachess brothers.

After I called Marley, I ordered Chinese and we ate in the lanai.

The weather was changing. There was a feeling of tension in the charged atmosphere; a sense of waiting descended as the languid feeling of tropical heat was replaced by cooler air. Over the pond a flash of lightning lit up the sky and a cool breeze blew through the screens.

I stood up and gathered the plates. "The weather is going to break at last." The first big drops of rain plopped on the brick path outside the lanai. "Let's take in the cushions before it happens."

During the night, thunderstorms shook the house and woke me from vivid nightmares. I got up and roamed the house in bare feet, thinking of things I had no answers to.

I stood at the living-room window and stared out into the violent night. More than one kind of evil was waiting in the dark for me.

CHAPTER 39

Aunt Kay called early the next morning. Maybe the change in the weather had energized her, or maybe it was the fear of what was yet to come for her, but she was eager to get started.

"We'll stay well away from the Vachess brothers, but we need to talk to the people who Holly worked with. That will be safe, won't it?"

"My truck is at the Sunset. I'm not going back there to pick it up so I have nothing to drive."

"It's all right, I have. My PT Cruiser is in the garage. I haven't been able to drive it since my troubles began."

"I'm not going near your place."

"Fine, but there's been no sign of anyone watching my house. My neighbor uses my vehicle now and then, when they need an extra car, and in return she takes me for groceries. I'll see if she'll drive me to that big Walmart Plaza on Forty-one. You can meet me there."

Brian and I had to drive around the enormous lot a couple of times before we found Aunt Kay.

"You're kidding, right?" I considered her ride. "It's purple."

"No it isn't. It's burgundy."

"Burgundy and ugly, but a great disguise. Ryan will never look for me inside a great big plum and with any luck, if our paths do cross, he'll think it's a hallucination."

"Such a precious little princess." Aunt Kay handed me the keys and a piece of paper. "That's the address of the place where Holly worked before the baby was born."

I peered in the window to make sure that there was a steering wheel, gearshift and all the other things a car normally has and not just a big pit, while the passenger door slammed behind Aunt Kay.

The Southgate Day Spa was in a small plaza on Tamiami Trail, standing all on its own away from the other stores as if to show it was a class beyond. The large windows were covered in gauzy curtains and the glass door was etched with a tropical design of palm branches so you couldn't see inside. The door opened into a small waiting area where a perfectly made-up receptionist talked quietly on a phone. Behind her the long line of manicurists, in identical white smocks, looked up expectantly as we came in. Nail grinders and buffers whirred and the smell of polish filled the air. The receptionist smiled and pointed to the gilt chairs lined up in front of the windows.

Aunt Kay plopped down. Six inches of her anatomy overflowed the chair on either side, but she planted her bag on her lap and sat there like this was the kind of place she came to every day.

Beside her, I picked up a brochure off a glass table. Rejuvenation treatments, massages, waxing and airbrush tanning, plus facials, makeup and nails, were all offered by the salon.

"Let's get a bikini wax," I whispered and pointed to a picture in the brochure I'd picked up off the table.

Aunt Kay didn't respond.

I nudged her. "There's something called a body polish. Funny, I never felt the need to polish my body, but there it is, one more way for me to fall short of someone else's expectations. 'Course, with your full figure, they'll have to charge you double, more area that needs polishing."

She huffed at me and stared straight ahead, so I took it that she wasn't interested in self-improvement and put the brochure back.

The receptionist was sweet and wanted to be helpful but she'd only been there since Christmas, so she went to find someone who might have known Holly. That person was Kerry, no last name, just Kerry. She was the manager and looked almost perfect, apart from the frown.

Aunt Kay told her about Holly's death and asked who Holly's friends were at the spa.

Kerry said, "We don't encourage staff to get friendly. It leads to cliques and factions and then there are problems in the workplace. It just doesn't work out."

Aunt Kay wouldn't let it go, asking more questions but getting no more information.

It wasn't that Kerry meant to be unhelpful, it was just that she had noticed very little that was personal about Holly, barely remembered her beyond her work record. Kerry wasn't interested in anything unless it added to the bottom line.

"Staff come and go pretty quickly here. Mind you, Holly stayed longer than the majority. I was sorry to let her go."

"Why did you fire her?" I asked.

Kerry jerked back. "I'm not sure . . . I don't want any trouble."

"We aren't here to stir up trouble for you, dear," Aunt Kay said.

Kerry worried her lip. "The wife of a famous producer comes in here. Holly went on and on about auditioning for him. The man's wife asked not to have Holly do her nails again. Then Holly got her number from the receptionist and called him at home. We can't have manicurists that do things like that. Besides, she was eight months pregnant." As soon as the words were out of Kerry's mouth, she screwed her lips shut into a hard knot.

I asked, "Did Holly come back with her baby?"

"God no. Why would she do that?"

"You're right," I said. "It would have been foolish."

My cell rang when we got back to the car.

The caller said, "It's Dan."

"What's up?"

He didn't speak.

"What is it, Dan?"

"It's . . . Holly."

"What?"

"I worked overtime this morning. Hung about and checked in with the lead detective, just casual, like I was interested because I found her. I asked about the autopsy."

I could hear Dan crying.

"What did the autopsy show?"

It took a while for him to answer. "Holly was HIV-positive."

"Sweet Jesus. Are you sure?"

"Don't be stupid," he yelled.

I swallowed and said, "What about you?"

"I'm leaving now to get tested. There's a new quick test they can do. They can tell in under an hour if the antibodies are there."

"I'm sorry." What else was there to say? "Dan, did the autopsy say she committed suicide?"

"She had enough pills in her system to kill her twice." His voice was harsh and low with emotion. "She was never going to wake up."

"What kind of drugs?"

"Oxycodone."

"Why that drug?"

"It's what every suicide I've ever been called out for uses." It sounded like he was struggling to breathe. "I don't care about Holly."

After a long silence, he said, "Don't you understand? I'm scared shitless. The report said that this is a new strain of HIV, one that moves quickly and is lethal. Oh my god, I could have given it to Shelly. Goddamn, Holly."

"Dan, Holly would never knowingly expose you to anything."

"Yeah, well, what if she didn't know she had it?"

And that was the kicker.

Dan said, "There's something more."

Why wasn't I surprised?

"Aunt Kay was right. The autopsy shows that Holly had given birth and the report also said she had a tattoo. I never saw any tattoo on her. It's new, a picture of wings with the word Angel underneath."

Lots of people have a tattoo with their kids' names, but the wings . . . that brought images of heaven. Had Aunt Kay's instincts been right? Did the wings mean Angel was dead?

"Ask at the hospital if Angel could have been born with HIV."

He moaned.

"Dan, do you want me to go with you?"

It took a bit of time for him to answer. "No."

"Call me when you know."

He hung up without replying.

Aunt Kay was staring at me as if I was an alien.

"Holly was HIV-positive."

She was shaking her head, her face white with shock.

"It's worse than that. Dan said it was a new and lethal strain. The question is does Angel have it? Aren't pregnant mothers tested for the HIV virus?"

We were silent for a moment and then Aunt Kay said, "Who could we ask?"

"I need a computer. We're going to Brian's."

"I was right," I said, reading the screen in front of me. "Pregnant women are tested at their first doctor's visit and again at twenty-eight to thirty weeks. Holly would know if she had the virus and she would know if Angel had been born HIV-positive."

Aunt Kay dug her fingers in her wooly hair. "Surely Holly would have told me if she was sick. She knew she could always come home to me."

"Holly didn't hint that she was ill?"

"Absolutely not. She could have moved in with me and looked after Angel for herself, but that wasn't what Holly wanted. She wanted someone to take Angel full-time. She had plans. She was quite upbeat and acting like something good was about to happen."

"Give me that picture of Angel."

Aunt Kay dug through her purse and handed the paper over.

I took it to Brian's copier while Aunt Kay stood at the window looking out towards the pond. "Let's go out, Sherri."

"There's a bull gator that lives out there. He's going to be moved this week but in the meantime I'm not going near the water."

She put both her hands on the glass and leaned forward. "I don't see him. Let's go outside."

Something was happening with Aunt Kay. She'd been silent all the way back to Jacaranda. It wasn't just the news about Holly. It was as if someone had turned off a light inside her, as if she were slipping away from me. She was frightening me but I didn't know what to do.

I went to stand beside her and had a good look along the water. "Okay, but if I see him, I'm ditching you and beating it back inside."

She clutched my arm with both hands as we made our way along the narrow brick path fronting the lanai. Breathing hard, like she couldn't get enough oxygen, she stopped often and lifted her face to the sun. "I love this."

We stepped onto the lawn and she paused. I dug my toes in the thick grass, so lush and deep that it felt more like a chenille bed-spread than anything natural.

"Do you know what I've discovered in the last sixty years?" she said, still with her face turned skyward.

She didn't really want an answer so I offered none.

"There's no such thing as safe. We can't make anyone safe, not even ourselves. Bad things happen. Cars crash and disease surprises us and no matter how much you want to save someone else it can't be done. Thinking we can help is just ego saying we know best."

I watched the water for any sign of the gator.

"I was just afraid of sitting around waiting for the end. I wanted to feel like I was doing something, and then I brought those brothers into your life."

"Let's go inside. It's too hot for you out here." I tried to turn her around.

She took no notice of me. "Doesn't matter anyway, only tempo-rary, it all ends the same. There is no happy ever after."

She looked at me, her face intense, her hands clutching me. "It's all rabbit's feet and knocking on wood. And prayer . . . but there's no one listening." Her lips quivered.

"Holly's death has been too much for you. This is shock and depression talking."

"Or sanity. I tell you, Sherri, I've had enough."

I felt her move slightly. Her eyes widened and she gave a gentle "Ah" of a sigh.

When the fire truck arrived, faster than I thought possible, I said, "She has a heart condition," and struggled to remember the name. My brain wouldn't work. "Something Wolfe."

The rescuer didn't look up from Aunt Kay. "Does she have medi-cation for it?"

"Yes."

"Get it."

"I'm not sure . . ." I left it at that and ran into the house for her purse.

I handed over a vial of pills. "Is she still . . ." I couldn't even finish the question.

He wrote down the information on the bottle and then handed me the pills. An ambulance arrived. The firefighters carried her towards the ambulance.

That's when I stopped believing Aunt Kay was exaggerating her heart problems. One more thing I was wrong about.

It had been my week for making mistakes.

CHAPTER 40

Waiting outside the ICU was about as comfortable as sitting inside a freezer in my underwear. A nurse saw me shivering and stopped to see if I was all right.

"Cold, very cold in here," I said between chattering teeth.

"I'll get you a blanket."

"Wait," I called. "When can I see Aunt Kay . . . Mrs. Fairchild?"

"I'll ask."

She came back with a flannel sheet and wrapped it around me. "I heated it."

"Heaven." I tried to smile.

"They're doing an echocardiogram," the nurse said. "You can see her shortly."

At least Aunt Kay was still alive. That was something.

It seemed forever before the door opened and the nurse said, "You can come in now."

Aunt Kay was hooked to a load of machinery that hummed and beeped. It was a world with no before and no after, just the here and now, marked by the immediacy of the pulse of a machine.

Aunt Kay's black, piercing eyes found me and she reached up to remove the oxygen mask. The nurse stopped her hand. "Leave it."

Aunt Kay looked like she wanted to argue.

"Leave it." I put my hand on her shoulder. "We'll talk tomorrow."

She closed her eyes.

The machines hummed on and the nurse left. Aunt Kay's eyes opened and the mask came down again. "I want you to . . ."

The machinery changed tempo.

"Shush," I put her oxygen mask back over her face and held her hand. I tried to pull my hand out of hers to get a chair, but she grabbed on tight and wouldn't release me. I hooked my right foot around the leg of the chair and dragged it closer so I could sit down. I held her hand and the machines beeped on.

When I left the hospital it had rained and stepping outside was like walking into a sauna. Steam rose from the pavement, the smell of it filling my nose and mixing with the odor of tar and dust. The drought might have lessened but the heat hadn't let up.

I called Clay and told him about Aunt Kay. Over and over during our conversation I said, "I'm fine." Why do we always say that? Just once I'd like to say, "I'm a walking basket case." Truthfully, I'm probably not a very good judge of my emotional state since I've spent so much of my life lying about it.

"We need to talk," Clay said.

"Not now." I'd had all the bad news I could handle for one day. "I can't think."

"Okay, just so you know it's coming."

Clay called Tully and he was at Brian's waiting for me when I got there. Tully was convinced I shouldn't be alone so he'd come to Brian's to check on me. Tully Jenkins, the beer-swigging, danger-loving man in the role of caregiver was an outlandish thought. I even thought Clay was crazy to leave Tully to look after the animals on the ranch. Perhaps Tully had changed, even if my view of him hadn't. He'd had a long adolescence, but perhaps maturity had finally found him. Not once in the last year had he disappeared without telling anyone where he was going and the all-night poker games seemed to be a thing of the past. Even his drinking was well within the world of normal.

Tully stared at me intently and then held out his hand. "Give me that phone thing."

I handed my cell over to him. "Why don't you just get one of your own?"

He held my cell at the end of his arm and squinted at it. "Don't need one."

"Only because you use everyone else's."

He leaned his head back and tried to lengthen his arm.

I retrieved my phone. "What number do you want?" He told me. I dialed it and then handed it to him.

"Hi Bernice," he said.

I left the room.

CHAPTER 41

Brian was already cooking dinner. I dipped a spoon into the pot of chili he was stirring. His face was beet red and sweat glued his shirt to his back. "What do you think? It's got chocolate in it."

"Best chili I ever tasted." I went to the cupboard and got down the bowls as Tully stuck his head in the door and said, "This thing is buzzing." He handed me my cell.

I left the kitchen, taking the bowls with me into the dining room, so I could talk to Marley in private.

I told her about Aunt Kay and then I said, "There's something else."

"What's that?"

"Clay may have taken up with Laura again. He says we have to talk."

Dead silence.

"Marley?"

"It can't be."

"Never bet against the stupidity of men."

"You only say that because of Jimmy. Jimmy would shag an alligator given half a chance. Clay is not Jimmy."

I set the bowls on table mats. "Laura's up in Cedar Key with Clay right now."

"How do you know?"

I told her. "Clay has a good reason for Laura being in Cedar Key

197

with him but I hear Miss Emma in my head saying, 'I ain't got no use for lame excuses.'" Miss Emma ran the Sunset when I first came back to Jac and every time someone was late or screwed up she'd say, "I ain't got no use for lame excuses. What I needs is bums in chairs and your feet on the ground running."

"You love Clay, don't you?" Marley asked.

"Yeah," I said and then I added, "but not like Jimmy."

"Thank god for that. No one should go insane twice. Clay's a great guy."

"And it's the best sex I've ever had."

"Another good thing. So fight for him."

"I may not get the chance."

"Want me to come into town?"

"Can you stop bad things from happening?"

"Nope."

"See, what I need is a superhero. Or maybe a magic potion."

"I haven't got one of those either."

"Well then, you don't need to come to Jac." I wiped my nose with the back of my hand. "Got it all under control."

"I've heard that before, usually right before you do something really stupid." There was a heartbeat of silence and then she added, "God, don't shoot Laura, will you?"

I wanted a long soak in a tub where no one could get at me.

Every day I identified more and more with Holly. Delving into her life had left me shaken and assessing my own situation in a new light. Like her, I always have this rock-firm belief that something will shake loose, something good will happen, even when past experience proves it isn't true. I hug my dreams close to me like a child with a stuffed animal, unwilling to give up on them like any sensible person would. If you give up on your dreams, what do you have left?

Just as I climbed into the tub my cell rang. I picked it up off the floor and checked. Marley was calling me back before the wave had ebbed on my descent into the water. I considered not answering but that would only piss her off. She doesn't like being ignored. "Yeah," I said.

"Start at the beginning and tell me everything."

"You already know everything."

"Pretend I don't. Make believe I'm slow and not the sharp woman I really am. Start with Aunt Kay showing up."

I started at the beginning. When I came to the part where Laura was up in Cedar Key and Clay had something to tell me but I didn't know what it was she said, "Shit." And then again, "Shit. This can't be happening."

"My sentiments exactly."

"Oh shit, Sherri. He wouldn't do that, would he?"

"He tells me Laura Kemp is there to decorate the model suites so he can sell them."

"Call him and tell him to get down here. You can't wait until he decides to tell you what's happening."

I used my toe to turn on the hot water. "Trust me, I can wait."

"Don't you want to know the truth?"

"In my opinion, truth is not necessary for a comfortable life. I've never been real fond of reality, and I have enough imagination to keep it at bay."

"Then call and tell him you're worried. You can at least do that, can't you?"

"Do you realize how much of my life takes place on a telephone?" I turned off the hot water. "Sometimes I just want to talk to him face to face, especially when it's something important. I'm not gonna call."

"Then just tell him you need him to get his ass back here. Tell him about Ryan. That'll get his attention."

"Nope."

"Why?"

"Because he already thinks I'm crazy."

"Well, so do I!"

"Not like Clay does. He hasn't come out and said it but he thinks I'm imagining things, thinks I need medical help. The only thing standing between me and some heavy therapy is my inability to pay."

"So you're just going to sit there and do nothing?"

"Seems like it."

"Honest to god, sometimes I think you've turned stupidity into an art form."

I sank down in the tub, letting the water lap up to my chin and listened to her lecture.

When she ran out of breath, I said, "And there's another thing I haven't told you about my week."

"No kidding? Better than this? I can't wait to hear it. What?"

I heard a voice from beyond the bathroom door. I sat up in the tub so fast a wave of water washed over the side. Marley started to ask a question but I went, "Shhh."

And there it came again, the voice I so didn't want ever to hear again.

CHAPTER 42

"Is that Bernice?" Marley whispered.

The horror I felt was reflected in Marley's voice, like I'd left the bathroom door open and Ted Bundy had snuck in.

Marley hissed, "What's she doing there?"

"Ah, that's the other thing I meant to tell you."

"What?"

"Bernice and Tully are having an affair."

A startled shriek came out of the phone followed by the oddest noises, like Marley was having some kind of a fit.

"I'm so glad you're enjoying this." I opened the drain. "If I got hit by a bus, I suppose you'd get a good laugh out of that too."

She couldn't answer.

I stood up and reached for a towel. "Now I'm going out there and I'm going to pour myself a really big glass of wine. Not even Tully can expect me to face that bitch sober."

The new Tully was convinced I was in shock and thought alcohol would be a bad idea. The old Tully would have raced me to the bottle.

God, it was awful. Bernice trying to be sympathetic and kind and all the time her eyes were on Tully, anxious and hanging on to his every word, watching him to see how all of this was going to play out for them. She was threatened.

I'd never seen a sign of weakness in her before. Not once, through Jimmy's drug use and scrapes with the law, or even his death. Bernice's strength came from her anger, holding it aloft like a torch to guide her, always finding someone else to blame for whatever trouble descended on them. Now this Amazon of a woman was quivering at the thought of losing my old man.

The truth jolted me. I felt a brief flame of power until I realized how ridiculous that made me, wanting to destroy my dad's happiness to get some kind of revenge on Bernice.

I wrapped Brian's terrycloth housecoat tighter around me and snugged up the belt. "Look, Tully, I'm in for the night. Actually I'm going off to bed early. Why don't you and Bernice take off?"

Tully's face was screwed up in concern. He was probably asking himself what a responsible adult would do in this situation.

I went to him and sat on the arm of his chair, wrapping my arms around his shoulders and kissing his cheek. "Thank you for being there for me, Dad, but you have to stop worrying now." I looked down into his face. "Take Bernice and go home."

"Are you sure?" He didn't quite believe I wasn't about to fall apart. It was like me not wanting to leave Aunt Kay, afraid if I stepped out of the hospital to make a call, something awful would happen.

I glanced at Bernice. Her face was lit up like Christmas and she was already halfway to her feet.

"I'm sure," I said.

I nodded to her and hugged Tully. "We'll talk in the morning."

When the door closed behind them, Brian said, "Well, that was sure disappointing. I thought the two of you would give a better show than that." And then he added, "Bernice was pretty happy to have Tully to herself, wasn't she?"

"Yup."

"She didn't like Tully rushing to your side, did she?"

"Nope." I headed for the kitchen and another glass of wine.

Brian followed me. "Is it because in a cat fight over Tully she knows she'd lose?"

"I don't know and I don't care. I'm too tired for a brawl or to even think about fighting."

Brian shook his head sadly. "Those are words I never thought I'd hear you say."

CHAPTER 43

The next morning Tully called while I was in Brian's kitchen pouring my first coffee. He seemed to think Bernice and I had turned a corner and were on the verge of being best friends. I was struck by an incredible vision of the future. "You don't expect me to be spending family time with her, do you . . . like sitting across the table from her at Thanksgiving dinner?"

"I'll get back to you on that," he said.

I didn't tell him in how many ways that wasn't going to happen.

But Tully was wise enough to change the subject. "You think they'll let Kay out today?"

"God, I hope not. She's depressed, doesn't seem to have any reason to live."

"Then give her one."

I didn't waste my breath asking how to do that because I already knew what Aunt Kay needed.

I went into Brian's office and found a magnifying glass, a cute little thing with a light, and examined the print from behind the fridge. The woman's face was still hidden by her hair but that didn't matter. It was her sleeve I was interested in. I could only read a bit. It said "Gor . . ." before the cloth folded. This was followed by the word "Studio."

Then I had it. I knew where Angel was. Ashley Gordon and I played volleyball together in high school and stayed friends. Josh and Ashley were going through in vitro fertilization while Holly was working at the Sunset. Holly knew all about the situation, everybody did. Ashley was in the Sunset a lot back then, drinking orange juice in case she might be pregnant, and hanging out because she and Josh were getting on each other's nerves. The in vitro had failed but Ashley still wanted a baby.

Ashley would be a terrific mom. Did I want to interfere in her life? If I got rid of the picture, no one would ever know where Angel was. But Josh and Ashley had to know about Holly's illness, to know that Holly was dead. I waffled back and forth trying to decide on the right thing. If I did nothing and Angel had the virus, the consequences could be enormous.

I tried to argue myself out of it. The bottom line, though, was they had to be told Holly wasn't coming back.

I asked Tully to drive me to the Sunset before it opened so I could do the payroll and pay the bills. He drove by twice, checking the vehicles. The only cars in the parking lot were the familiar cars of staff, doing prep work and getting ready for the day.

Tully came up the stairs with me and I pretended I didn't know what he was hiding under the cowboy shirt he had pulled out of his jeans. No way was I going to get picky about Tully carrying a concealed weapon with Ryan on the loose.

I checked invoices, including a wine bill I was sure had to be wrong but which I had a strong suspicion was accounted for by my own drinking habits. I finished what was necessary in the way of bookwork to keep things functioning, shuffling bills around and lying to a few people about when their checks would arrive. Then I talked menus with Miguel over coffee and muffins. When the door closed behind him my cell rang.

I picked it up and checked the name.

"Hey, babe," Clay said.

That's all it took for me to know what was coming. "Tell me," I said.

"Don't rush it."

"Screw the foreplay, Adams, and tell me."

He laughed, crazy, mad and delighted.

"I've got an offer—more than that, a signed contract, and there's even enough left on the table for us to have a new start."

"Oh god. Is it really done?"

"I've got their names on the dotted line and a check in my pocket. I'm almost on my way home."

"Well, you hurry on down here so we can start celebrating."

"Aah," he said.

"I don't like the sound of that."

"I can't make it until later in the week. I've got some things to clean up. I don't want to come home and then turn around and come back—Sunday for sure. And I've got a plan. I'm going to be the new tenant on the ground floor of the Sunset. I'm going to open my real estate office again. You are going to be so sick of seeing my face." He laughed. "I'll tell you all about it when I get there."

"Okay, I can wait that long. But you better get here before dinner on Sunday or come wearing armor."

"Honey, I'm already packing. There's something else . . ." He cleared his throat. "I'm not very good at this. For now, I just want you to know that I love you more than my very breath."

Tears pricked my eyes and my voice went husky. "I think you're doing just fine."

CHAPTER 44

I put Aunt Kay's check in the bank and then I went to see her. She looked better, but her spirits hadn't improved.

"What do you want me to do today?"

Aunt Kay's lips pursed. "Maybe it's time we minded our own business."

"Well, that's up to you, but I don't give rebates."

She almost smiled.

"You're giving up?"

She turned her face away from me.

"After all we've done, you're calling it quits?"

"It's better that way," she told the wall.

"Well, I'm not quitting until I find Angel or run out of places to look."

"Why do you care?" She turned to look at me now. "You're only doing it for the money and I don't want it back."

"I'm not ready to give up. So you just lie there and forget Angel if you want, but I'm not going to."

She frowned.

I went to the bed and bent over her, my lips up close to her ear. I whispered, "I know where Angel is."

"Where?"

I grinned and said, "I thought you weren't interested." I headed for the door.

Ashley's studio was on Palmetto. Even before I got to the door and read the paper taped to the glass, I knew the dance studio was out of business. There was no suggestion as to when, or even whether, it might open again.

Ashley lived within walking distance, only a few blocks away in a small Spanish house built in the twenties, but it was just too damn hot to walk.

When I pulled into the driveway the first of my questions was answered. A stroller sat beside the little stoop of the pretty house with a FOR SALE sign on the lawn.

I bent over and picked up a small white lamb from the front step. The little toy was silky in my hand, soft and yielding as I ran my palm over it. Birds sang and screams of delight came from kids enjoying a pool somewhere close. Nothing bad could ever happen here. All I had to do was drive away.

I pressed the doorbell.

Ashley opened the door and her face lit up. "Sherri!" She stepped back and held the door wide. "Come in." A little cherub, with auburn curls, rode her left hip.

I'd been a serious underachiever in high school while Ashley was the girl who did it all. Student council, cheerleader and A student, Ashley worked hard at everything and was always perfect. Today, her hair was pulled back in a ponytail and she wore no makeup, unheard of for the Ash I knew.

The child reached out for me with both hands. My heart fluttered and I responded by opening my arms, but it was the toy she wanted, not me. She grabbed it in her hands and drew it to her mouth with a yelp of delight.

"It was on the ground," I said, ready to take it away from her.

"No worries." Ashley laughed. "Lily is immune to dirt." She pivoted back into the room, moving with the grace of the dancer she'd been since childhood. "Come on in and ignore the mess. I've learned to."

She was right, the place was a disaster. Toys and baby equipment were everywhere and you could no longer see the beautiful arched plaster fireplace Ashley had been so proud to own. Two upholstered chairs had been pushed together in front of the fireplace to protect a curious toddler from the danger of falling on the raised marble hearth. All the wrought-iron furniture was gone and the white sectional was covered with old limp quilts, collapsing down the back onto the seat cushions.

From house proud to home disaster, all in one small bundle but Ashley was happier than I'd ever seen her. She didn't question why I was there, just nattered nonstop about feeding and diapers and all sorts of things, events that seemed world-shatteringly important to her, pleased to see an old friend and have a little relief from her routine. Most of all she talked about how much she loved Lily.

Ashley handed Lily to me while she went to make coffee. Lily's soft reddish curls brushed against my face. The eyes she turned up to me were blue, just like Holly's. And Sunny was right, Lily's mouth was a perfect rosebud.

She took being hugged by a stranger as a normal occurrence, alternating between chewing on the lamb and pounding it on her lap. Once in a while she stopped to tug on the gold chain I was wearing.

I couldn't bring myself to mention my reason for visiting in front of Lily. She wouldn't know what we were saying but it just wouldn't be right.

"How come you're moving?" I asked as Ashley sank onto a chair across the table from me.

"Josh has a great job offer in Tallahassee but the house hasn't sold." She gave a wry little laugh. "Don't know why. We've got it in showroom condition."

"It must be impossible to show a house with a baby." I laid my cheek against the silky curls.

"Yeah, the minute the realtor calls and says he's bringing someone by I start running around cleaning. Lily comes right behind me and it's undone as fast as I fix it. And of course, every three seconds you have to pull her away from something."

"Maybe I could come over and take Lily for a walk while you get ready for the showing." The offer popped out of my mouth before I even thought about it.

"Oh, Sherri, would you really?"

"Sure."

Lily yawned.

"About time too," Ashley said and plucked Lily out of my arms. "Be right back."

Lily watched me over her mother's shoulder, one plump little arm bouncing up and down almost as if she were waving goodbye.

"I have something to tell you," I said when Ashley returned.

She went to the coffee pot. "What's up?"

"Holly Mitchell is dead."

The carafe slammed back into its holder. The face she turned to me was full of alarm but she didn't ask why I was telling her this. "What happened to her?"

"She committed suicide last Sunday."

She gasped and covered her mouth with both hands.

I went to her and led her back to the table. I picked up the coffee pot and filled our cups. She sat across from me in total shock.

"Lily is Holly's baby, Angel, isn't she?"

She nodded.

"There is something you have to know." I reached out for her hands and took them in mine. "Holly was HIV-positive."

It hurt to see her face.

"Listen to me, listen. From what I read online, the prenatal testing Holly got before Lily was born would have shown if Holly was HIV-positive. Holly would never have kept that from you. I don't think Holly contracted the virus until after Lily was born."

There was no need for me to tell Ashley to get Lily tested. She'd be on to the pediatrician before I was out of the drive.

"How on earth did you end up with Lily?"

She pulled her hands away from mine and took a deep breath. "I met Holly up at a mall in Sarasota. She had Lily with her. She asked if the in vitro had worked. It hadn't and I told her we were waiting to hear about getting a baby from China. It's such a long process. I told her I had everything, a crib, changing table, diapers, but no baby. She called a few days later and asked if I could keep Angel for her. I said yes. I thought it would be like a practice run but right away it got serious. Josh and I both fell in love with Lily and every time the phone rang we thought it was Holly wanting her back."

Tears ran down her face, silently and unheeded. "Last week Holly called and told us we could keep Lily forever."

"Did she tell you why?"

"She said she was sick and wouldn't be able to look after Lily. She asked if we would go to a lawyer and have legal papers for Lily's adoption drawn up for her to sign. We went up to Sarasota last Friday and met her in a coffee shop."

Her voice broke. "She signed the papers and gave us a letter to give to Lily when she grew up."

"Did she tell you anything else?"

"She told us Dan Raines was the father. She said he didn't know about the baby, said Dan had a baby the same age. She didn't want him to know about Lily right now, said Lily could tell him when she was ready."

CHAPTER 45

My cell rang as I walked to the truck.

"Hi," Dan said.

"You got good news."

He laughed. "I had the antibody test. It was negative."

"Does that mean you're safe?"

"Yup, I'd have it by now."

"I'm glad, Dan. Now you can get on with your life."

"I intend to. I was scared shitless. I'm going to be the most faithful husband in the world."

I opened the door and threw my bag in. "I still don't get how you came to be the one who found Holly."

He sighed. "She kept calling my cell that day. Told me she had to talk to me, insisted I call her. I ignored her calls. She called again, around suppertime, sounding pretty desperate, said she had something important to tell me. I was afraid if I didn't talk to her she'd call the house. When I took a break I was at a gas station and there was a public phone outside the washroom. I just wanted to tell her to stop calling me. I called her but she didn't answer. I called the station, made an anonymous call, knowing that, as the car in place, I'd be the one sent to check it out. She was dead when I got there. I checked the apartment to make sure there was nothing to tie me to her. There wasn't. It was really clean, everything packed up. She used to keep a journal but I couldn't find it. What do you suppose happened to that? Maybe she put it in the garbage."

"Or maybe someone else did."

"Whatever. She'd cleaned everything out, looked like she was moving or something. Doesn't matter now. She sure didn't leave anything behind. I'm safe."

And that's all that mattered to him—he was safe. Angel, Holly, well, they were just by-products of his happiness. His world was fine.

"Dan, can you find out about a guy named Ryan Vachess for me?"

"No." The volume of his response had me holding the phone away from my ear.

Silence stretched between us as we both got control of our anger. Finally, he said, "What about the baby, did you find her?"

"No. Apparently Holly gave her baby up for adoption. It probably was a private arrangement. It doesn't look like Holly told anyone who the baby went to. Everything to do with Angel is a deep dark secret. Even her own mother didn't know Holly had a child."

I dug my keys out of my pocket. "Seems Holly could keep things quiet when she wanted to, so you're off the hook." I didn't even try to hide my bitterness.

"I'd do the right thing if the child is alone."

"Forget it. Holly already did the right thing. Get on with your life. You have a family to look after."

"Does this guy, Vachess, have anything to do with the baby?"

I was surprised he remembered the name. "No, he's just someone Holly knew."

"Okay, but there's something else from the autopsy." He sounded reluctant and unsure, like maybe he would regret telling me.

"I hate to think what else could've happened to Holly."

"Holly was using crystal meth."

"It's too damn depressing. Addiction, giving up her child, and HIV? She sure had enough reasons to head for the door."

"There's one more."

I waited.

"Sherri . . ." He sounded like he was about to say more than he wanted to, more than he should. "The name of the guy who was paying for Holly's apartment is Dusty Harrison."

I'd forgotten about Dusty. "Why are you telling me?"

"I've been wondering if Harrison gave Holly HIV."

"Why do you care?"

"C'mon, I had feelings for Holly, but I was terrified of losing my wife and my job. Maybe even my life."

"So now all that's safe, why don't you go ask Harrison if he infected Holly?"

"I can't afford to. I get caught running around asking about a dead girl . . . well, it wouldn't do my career any good."

"Best not to then."

"Still . . . see what you can do, Sherri."

"Not much I can do—or want to do."

"You can talk to him in a language he's sure to understand."

"What makes this my job?"

"Holly had been systematically beaten over a long period of time. If he was the one keeping her he probably was the one beating on Holly for fun. If for no other reason, ruining Dusty's day will make the trip worthwhile."

Rage jolted me. "Now that sounds like a good time. Where do I find this bastard?"

"Got a pencil?"

"Just happens that I do."

CHAPTER 46

Only rich people live on Lido Key . . . not moderately wealthy people, but the filthy rich kind like Dusty Harrison.

The house on the bay, facing Sarasota across the water, was well back from the street. The black wrought-iron gates, designed to look like a piece of sheet music, stood open. If I could read music I bet the gates held the stupid Christmas tune that had paid for all this estate.

In this neighborhood there was sure to be private security. Thick plantings lined the curving drive and concealed the house, but I saw no signs of any security, nothing to stop me entering the grounds. I followed the drive to where it curled around a fountain in front of the house. On either side of the front door, the yews continued the musical theme, cut into the shape of treble clefs.

At the front door I saw the first signs of security—cameras mounted on the house. Still, it wasn't much.

The fury that had brought me here was fading. I was beginning to think confronting Harrison wasn't a good idea, telling myself that Holly was dead and nothing could change that. Still, all the things she'd suffered? I wanted some revenge for her pain.

I pushed the doorbell and the first bars of Dusty's Christmas song trilled. The sound brought back enough outrage to keep me committed.

The old woman who opened the door had pasted her lipstick well outside the natural lines of her lips, and it was even redder than what I wore. Her eyebrows were long gone but they'd been painted in thick black lines about an inch above where nature intended. Her clothes shimmered and still had shoulder pads; back in the eighties she would have been right in style.

She gave me the once-over, considered me from my head to my toes and back again. Her sour look said she was not impressed.

I put on my biggest smile. "May I speak to Mr. Harrison, please?"

"What's this about?" Her glare would have given a more sensitive type the jitters. "My son doesn't like girls like you."

"I'm afraid I have some sad news for him about a mutual friend."

"Tell me. I'm his mother."

"I think it's better if I tell Mr. Harrison."

"Dustin doesn't need to know. I don't want him upset," she said, and started to close the door.

A normal person might take a hint when a door is shut in her face. But I had Bernice to educate me and destroy any silly ideas of proper behavior. I slammed into the door with my shoulder, nearly knocking the old sweetheart on her ass. She recovered quickly, raising her hand and snarling, "Get out of my house."

"Would you rather he talked to me or the police?"

For a moment I thought she was going to rake her vivid red talons across my face.

The nails stopped reaching for me and a calculating look narrowed her eyes.

"It's his choice, but one way or another, my questions will get answered. However, the police might just want to take some actions beyond what I'm here for."

She squinted down her nose at me, judging if I were tough enough to make good on my words. "Wait in there," she said, pointing to a small den off to her left.

"Thank you."

Her nostrils flared.

"It really would be better if he talked to me instead of the police."

She tottered away on her toes, her gold lamé outfit flickering in the sunlight pouring through a glass dome over our heads.

The question was would she call my bluff? Who would come, Dusty or the cops?

I went to wait in the room she had pointed out. It was full of oversized furniture, looking rather like giant leather marshmallows.

The man who came was in his fifties with hair as black as his mother's. The color might well have come out of the same bottle. But where her face was prune-like, his was a smooth peach without a wrinkle or an expression in sight.

I rose to my feet when he entered the room, keeping the pepper spray hidden in my hand.

He stopped just inside the door and looked me up and down. His nose twitched as though his cat had dragged in something ghastly and he wanted the help to come and take it away. "What do you want?"

"I'm here about Holly."

"I don't know to whom you are referring."

"Then I'll take my questions to the police."

His large sigh was dramatic. "What questions?"

"You kept Holly in an apartment. I know that because the police told us. Were you the father of her child?" I was trying to throw him off guard. It didn't work.

He giggled . . . a horrible sound. "I didn't even know she had a child. I've only known her for a few months." He had a self-satisfied smirk on his face, sure that he knew where this was going and that he was free of any nasty paternity suit. "Besides, not that it's any-one's business, but I made sure years ago that I would never spawn anything."

"Thank god for that! And spawn was exactly the word I would have chosen. Was she leaving you?"

Dusty snickered. His amusement was really pissing me off.

"I told her to get out. She was really rather boring. She never stopped going on about when was I going to introduce her to some important people. Blathering on and on about her career. Besides, she wasn't . . ." He paused and looked at me. "Well, shall I say, she wasn't very enthusiastic in bed. She was starting to turn me off and I'd had enough of her. I told her she had two weeks to get out." His lips squeezed shut in disgust. "Stupid little fool went and killed herself."

"Did you give her drugs?"

"Never. I've never needed them."

"Bully for you, but you were the one who beat her."

His body stiffened. He gave a sniff.

"So, is that how you get your jollies, beating helpless women?"

He pointed at the door. "Get out."

"Not yet. We're not done. Did Cal Vachess hook you up with her?"

"Cal Vachess?" His confusion couldn't show on his face but it was there in his voice.

"Angel Escort, that's where you met her, right?"

"I don't need to use escort services." He was indignant at the suggestion.

"Ah," I said, nodding. "It had to be Ryan. That's how you met Holly."

"So? It was between consenting adults and no one's business."

I moved a little closer to him, wanting to see the fear in his eyes when I gave him the news. "So, here's a hot news flash . . . Holly was HIV-positive. With any luck you'll have it too."

Not all the Botox in the world could keep the fear off his face.

He pulled back his hand to slap me, but when a girl grows up in a trailer park she isn't an easy target. I dodged his hand and did exactly what Tully had taught me to do when I was about five.

Dusty hit the floor, groaning and clutching his crotch as he rolled onto his side.

I leaned over him. "Now mind your manners or I'll really hurt you. I'm betting you like to dish it out but you can't take it, is that right, Dusty?"

He didn't answer.

I nudged his back with my toe. "Talk to me here, Dusty."

"Yes," he gasped. "Don't hurt me."

"You were the one who beat Holly, weren't you?"

"Yes." Dusty's face was a funny color.

I had my pepper spray ready. "Get to your knees very slowly."

He moaned but he got to all fours. I grabbed his hair to pull up his head. The hair came off in my hand.

"Oh shit." I dropped the thing on the floor. "Shit," I said again and wiped my hand on my skirt. "That's just gross."

Behind me the door opened and Dusty's mommy came in.

"Dustin?" She tottered over and picked up the hair. Glaring at me, she said, "What have you done?"

Mrs. Harrison didn't wait for my answer. She was trying to put the toupee back on Dusty's head while he pushed her away. "Get out of here. Go away, Ma."

She started to do what she was told, turned back to offer him his hair, but finally clasped it to her chest and said, "I don't like that tone of voice, Dustin."

"Get out of here and mind your own business," Dusty screamed.

As she left the room, Dusty pulled himself into a crouch and crab-walked to a velvet wingback, collapsing into it. His face was wet with tears. I can't say they made me feel bad.

"You beat Holly for fun."

He watched me, his eyes locked on me.

"Tell me."

When he answered, the tone of his voice had changed, gone from aggressive to whining. "She liked it rough."

"Horseshit. You liked it rough."

He watched me warily, tears slipping down his cheeks.

"Did Ryan share your pastimes?"

"We partied together, if that's what you mean, but he lied to me, told me Holly was clean and safe."

"Don't you hate it when people lie to you?"

What would Aunt Kay want from him? "Holly needs to be buried and there's no money for a funeral. I want you to make out a check for ten thousand dollars."

He started to argue.

"I don't want Holly's name dragged through the mud, so your dirty little secret won't show up all over the Internet." I lifted the can of pepper spray and pointed it at him. "Do this one decent thing; it's best for everyone."

He held his hands up in appeasement. "All right, all right."

Wincing and moaning, he got to his feet. Sweat glistened on his face and his naked head. He walked slowly to the desk, leaning on it when he got there. Then he sat down gingerly and pulled himself forward. He hesitated. His hand slid towards the phone.

"Go ahead," I told him. "I'd like you to have me charged. I'd be happy to tell the cops and the reporters all about it. Tell them how Old Dusty, South Florida's pride and joy, likes beating up helpless women. You can sure as hell bet that I'll never have to hear your stupid Christmas song playing in any mall again. That would be a bonus."

He reached for a drawer instead of the phone and pulled out a long, red-leather checkbook.

"Make it out to Marnie Mitchell. And if you have second thoughts about this check after I've gone, think again." I gave him a big smile. "I've been on my best behavior today, didn't even bring any of my friends with me."

Dusty wrote and then held out the check.

I read what he'd written before tucking it into my bag. Then I pulled out Chloe McCabe's picture. "Do you know her?"

He squinted at the picture. He looked up at me, considering my face before he said, "I don't want any problems with Ryan Vachess."

"Don't worry about Ryan. It's me you've got a problem with."

"She was Ryan's and then she disappeared. I asked about her, thought I might like a turn, but he said she'd . . ." He stopped. His mouth twitched. "I don't want any trouble with Ryan."

"Better you worry about me."

"He said she was working on the road and then he laughed."

"What does that mean, working on the road?"

"Ryan has connections. Some guys have motor homes and their girls work out of them up and down the state, in truck stops and rest stops. They keep the girls high and keep them moving."

"Do you know where Chloe is now?"

He shook his head. "That's all I know about her."

I was barely out of the gate when I heard the sirens. Had to be his mother; for sure Dusty didn't want to bring the police into it and risk me telling them Holly's story.

CHAPTER 47

I figured by this time tomorrow Dusty would have left for a long vacation, so I drove to the deli to tell Rob what Dusty had said about Chloe. If he wanted to talk to Dusty or send the police to talk to him he'd have to hurry.

It was a hard, ugly thing to tell him, but Rob's reaction was pure excitement. "At least we know she's alive. Eighteen months without a word, I'd given up."

I dodged people coming into the deli without paying attention to my surroundings. It was a mistake. I should have had my head up and been looking out for a place to hide. Better still, I should have run back inside and started hollering "Help."

I felt his hand biting into my forearm, smelled the overpowering aftershave, before I registered Ryan Vachess's presence.

I didn't have time to think or react before he shoved me down into his car parked at the curb and then followed me inside it, slamming the door shut behind him.

I fell across the console with Ryan on top of me, squeezing my arm so hard it brought tears to my eyes. The fingers of his left hand dug into my hair and he jerked my head up to his face.

"Why are you following me?"

". . . wasn't following you."

He twisted his fingers in my arm. "Yes you were."

". . . coming out of the deli.".

"Yeah?" He shook my head. "Why that deli?"

His fingers locked into my jaw and cranked my head around. I gurgled an answer. He let go of my face and hissed, "You're in it with him."

Panicked, I said, "What the hell are you talking about?" I wanted to convince Ryan that my being there had nothing to do with him. "It's the only deli on St. Armand's. What deli should I have been coming out of?"

His face was up against mine. His breath was disgusting.

He moved slightly, settling onto the passenger seat but not releasing me. "What am I going to do with you now?"

I tried to scoot to the other side of the car and out the door. I didn't get far.

The nails of his right hand bit into the muscle of my upper arm. With his left hand he grabbed me by the hair and pulled me back. "You're not leaving until I say, bitch."

"You're hurting me."

He twisted my face around to his.

My fingers frantically searched for the zipper of my purse, desperate to get at the pepper spray. The animal cunning of a hyena flashed in his eyes. "What have you got in there?" He grabbed my bag and dropped it on the floor. "This is about those girls, about Chloe and Holly, isn't it?"

"Forget about Holly." My voice trembled with fear. "I have."

The bright and shiny pinpoints of his eyes were inches from my own. He said, "She just wouldn't give it up. Going on about it being my fault and how I had to look after her now, filling up my cell with messages and then slipping that note under my door." He slammed my head against the steering wheel. "She threatened me. No one threatens me."

"Please," I begged.

A smile, twisted and evil, curled his lips. "Stupid bitch would swallow anything she was handed. Just tell her the pills would stop the disease and make her feel better and she lapped them right up."

Suddenly the anger was gone and he was happy, a kid with a new trick. "No one can ever prove a thing. She just took them down like a good little girl."

He put his cheek right up against mine and whispered, "Good little girls are always the best, much more fun than the foul pieces of puke like you."

He pushed me out at arm's length and slammed me against the window. "Now what am I going to do with you?"

He didn't get a chance to make plans. The door opened and he was dragged backwards onto the sidewalk.

Suddenly free, my one thought was to get away. I grabbed my bag, digging in it for the spray, and stepped out into traffic. A horn blasted.

I shot my hand out as if I could stop the vehicle from running me down and wobbled around to the front of Ryan's car to the curb.

A woman started screaming.

On the sidewalk Ryan was curled up in a small ball to protect himself from Rob McCabe, who was cursing and kicking Ryan, apparently intent on killing him.

Two men grabbed Rob, pulling him back from Ryan, while other bystanders helped Ryan stagger to his feet. Blood ran down his face but Ryan pushed his rescuers away and scrambled into his Mustang. Pulling into traffic, he nearly collided with a gray Ferrari.

Rob reached out a shaking hand to me. "Are you all right?"

I couldn't answer.

"Come on." Rob took my hand and led me like a child back through the deli to the little room behind the counter. "Sit." He shoved me down onto the chair and left me there, returning within seconds with a mug of steaming coffee. "Drink this. I loaded it up with sugar. It'll help."

I wrapped my hands around the mug. Suddenly it didn't matter that it was ninety out. I needed the warmth and the comfort.

"We have to call the cops," Rob said.

"I don't know." I fingered the bump growing on my head. "Will they put him in jail?"

"Until his lawyer gets there."

"Then forget it. If they only put him away for a few hours it will be worse when he gets out."

Rob pulled up a small stool and sat facing me with our knees almost touching and studied me as if he expected me to faint. I wasn't sure it wouldn't happen.

I set the mug down. "It was the surprise. I didn't see him and then he had me in the car. And . . . oh my god, I think, I think . . ." But I couldn't say it, not to this man who was already carrying enough pain, couldn't tell him Holly hadn't committed suicide.

I asked, "How did you know?"

"I saw that stupid car. I came out to . . . well . . . I saw the two of you inside."

"Thank god. I am not sure how it would have turned out if you hadn't showed up. I might have been one more woman who disappeared from Ryan Vachess's life."

Rob got to his feet and pounded his fist on the wall. "Sometimes I think I'd be doing the world a favor if I just got a gun and shot him."

"Don't do it until you find Chloe."

I stopped rubbing the lump on my head and looked at Rob hard. For one second I was tempted to manipulate Rob into destroying Ryan. It wouldn't take much and if Ryan had it in for me before today, he was going to hate me even more now that he'd confessed to murder.

"You already told me your parents need you." I couldn't look at Rob. "Ryan's about to self-destruct."

"But how and when? And how many more women are going to get hurt?"

I folded my arms across my chest and leaned forward on my knees. "You need to find Chloe." And I needed to be alone.

He reached down and picked up the mug. "I'll call the police and tell them what Dusty Harrison said."

I nodded. "Do it quick before Dusty leaves town."

Rob put his hand on my shoulder and leaned towards me, earnest and concerned. "Why did Vachess pull you into his car?"

"He's paranoid and crazy, thinks I'm following him. He saw me coming out of here and thought it was part of a conspiracy."

The door was open to a small washroom, just a sink and a toilet. I stood up and went over to the sink and washed my hands and then my face. I pulled a handful of paper towels off a roll and dried my face before turning back to Rob. "He scares the shit out of me."

"Look, I'll come to the police with you. I'll tell them he was holding you in the car against your will."

I had something else in mind. Heaven help me, one day I'll grow a brain and the world will be a better place.

I pulled down on the denim skirt riding up over my ass and said, "Let me make a call first."

I figured I needed less orthodox help and I figured I knew where to get it. "It'll be okay. You go ahead, I'll be right out."

He went to the door to the alley, his phone already in his hand. "I'm calling the police about Chloe."

Hiding there in the back of the deli, while Rob called the cops, I called Dan.

"Ryan Vachess murdered Holly," I said as soon as he answered.

I told Dan about being hijacked and repeated Ryan's confession. I didn't get the response I had expected. I thought Dan's explosive temper would send him after Ryan. Instead Dan said, "It's over. Holly's death has been put down as a suicide. Leave it at that."

I was stunned. "Even if he killed Holly, you're willing to let it go?"

"You're just guessing."

"I'm not just guessing. He told me. I'll testify."

"Hearsay evidence, it won't stand up in court."

"When did you turn into such a wimp?"

"Since I got a life. Shelly and Hannah will be home tonight. They're all I care about now."

"Well, what about this—Ryan is knowingly infecting women with HIV. That's how Holly got the poison in her veins."

"You don't know that," Dan said.

"I think it will be pretty easy to prove. Diseases have profiles. He had the disease when he first met Holly. He knew he was going to make her sick and he didn't care."

"Intent is a hard thing to establish. He'd be in and out of custody the same day. Plus there's no longer a victim. Holly is dead."

"Dusty probably has it. He's a victim."

"You think Dusty Harrison is going to have his perverted sex life come out by charging Vachess? Not likely. Just drop it."

"You loved Holly a little. Are you going to let Ryan Vachess get away with this?"

"You're asking me to destroy my life. I'm not going to end my career to give Vachess a slap on the wrist. Forget about it, Sherri."

"What about the note?"

"What about it?"

"Something bothered me about that note, like a small stone in my shoe. It just kept irritating me. I got Aunt Kay to copy it out for me and her note had the same mistake in it as the one you wrote. The first word of the suicide letter wasn't capitalized. It looked like it was the beginning of a sentence but it wasn't. It said, '. . . because my Angel is gone.' It was the middle of a line. Ryan used the second page of her letter as a suicide note."

"And that's it? You think that's enough to get a guilty verdict?"

"It's right there in black and white, proof."

"The defense will argue she was about to kill herself, not surprising if she slipped up and didn't use a capital letter."

"Things like that are habits. You don't make that kind of a mistake."

"It isn't enough. Can you prove Vachess ever saw that note? Can you prove any of this shit you're telling me?"

"You could if you did your job."

"It's going to be your word against his. Don't get me involved."

"Please, Dan, for Holly's sake."

"I want to forget I ever knew her," he said, and then he hung up on me.

A tsunami of anger swamped me and I cursed Dan. He was supposed to serve and protect, isn't that what cops always said? But he was leaving Ryan on the street.

All those times he said Holly had called him and he hadn't got back to her. Had she been calling him for help, trying to get away from Dusty and Vachess?

CHAPTER 48

How many days had it been since I first heard the name Ryan Vachess? Three, no, it had been four days since my world imploded. And how many days would it be before I got it back again? But Ryan Vachess had to be stopped.

The man was a walking time bomb set to go off in my direction, not only paranoid but now he'd be afraid I'd go to the police and tell them he killed Holly. He wasn't going to let me walk around knowing that, but Dan was right, it would be my word against his. Would my word be enough?

Cautiously, I left the deli with Rob beside me. There was no sign of Ryan. Rob walked me to my truck and stood on the sidewalk and watched with his cell phone in his hand, his face creased with concern.

My pepper spray was on my lap and my cell was open on the seat beside me. I drove out of St. Armand's Circle, checking the traffic around me. Not seeing a red Mustang did not make me feel safe. Ryan might have changed cars. Rob pulled out of a side street and in behind me to follow me back over the bridge to the mainland and north on Tamiami Trail.

It didn't matter how it turned out, I wanted Ryan's crimes on record, wanted to stand up and say what he'd done. Someone else would decide if they believed me and if he was going to jail for what he'd done to Holly. That wasn't my responsibility. My only part in this was to tell what I knew and try to get justice for Holly.

With Rob following me I headed for the Sarasota police head-quarters on Adams Lane, north of Payne Park. I'd been there once before, in my life with Jimmy, when I was still running to his rescue and still believing he would change.

The Sarasota police headquarters looks like a blue plastic storage box that someone cut window slits in and topped with a sheet of glass.

Rob went to put in a report on Chloe while I waited in a tiny room to talk to an investigator in the Crimes Against Persons Unit. It took some time before a detective named Benning came to talk to me. She was very polite and listened to my story without interruption but gave absolutely no indication if she believed me or not. "And the brother, Cal Vachess, conspired in Holly's murder. I think he destroyed the journals and cleaned up after his brother fed her the pills."

Benning's eyes got big when I told her about being at Dusty's house. My account seemed impossible even to my own ears. "Rob McCabe will back up my story of Ryan Vachess holding me in the car." I handed over Rob's card and she took it without comment. "He's here in the building making a report on his sister Chloe."

By the time I was done I thought it was going nowhere, that she would put me down as one more crazy woman with an ax to grind. After she'd heard the whole story she politely asked me to wait and went away.

The adrenaline and the telling had dulled the sharpness of my fury. Now, exhausted, I just wanted to go back to Brian's and sleep until Clay came home to hold me.

I waited. People going by the cell-like interview room peered in the open door and took a good look at me for future reference. I ignored them and slumped down in the chair, trying to get comfort-able, and then I folded my arms on the desk and put my head down. I was drifting in and out of sleep when Officer Benning came back into the room.

Her attitude had changed. Before she even sat down across from me she said, "Are you willing to bring charges against Ryan Vachess for your illegal confinement?"

So they weren't going to arrest him for murder or spreading a disease. I took a deep breath. "Yes, I'll swear out a complaint for kidnapping me."

"Good." Her smile brightened the room.

"What about Dan Raines?"

"Oh, don't worry; we'll take care of Officer Raines."

I nodded. Dan should have shown a little more compassion for Holly.

It took some more time to swear out a complaint. I knew it would only slow Ryan down for about half a second but it might give the police leverage.

When it was done she said, "I'll call you as soon as we pick Ryan Vachess up." She stood up and held out her hand. "Don't worry, he won't hurt you now."

I wished I could be as hopeful as she was that my problems were over.

When I turned on my cell outside the station there were two calls from Ryan Vachess. He'd heard from Dusty. Both of the calls used words that were neither nice nor complimentary. He did not leave a number nor did he suggest I call him back. That was fine with me. I had all the friends I could handle. And, since I was sure that what he suggested was physically impossible, and might injure me if I tried, I decided to ignore his advice.

One thing was clear. Ryan made no mention of being worried about contracting the virus—that didn't come up in all the vile things he said in his messages—so he already knew Holly had HIV and didn't need me or Dusty to tell him. I didn't erase the calls. I saved them to play for the police. But not now. I was well and truly done. I had one more stop and then I was going back to Brian's to crash.

There was no sign of Rob but his car was still right beside my pickup. I figured I'd catch up with him later. I hit the freeway and headed south, back to Jacaranda.

At the hospital Aunt Kay was in a real room with real walls instead of curtains. It even had a window. She was sitting up in bed and she'd lost that dead fish look.

She brushed my questions about her health aside and said, "Where's Angel?"

I told her that Angel was now called Lily and I told her about Lily's wonderful home.

Her lips trembled. "Thank you, Sherri."

"You're welcome." I pulled a chair up to the bed. "I met Dusty Harrison. It was most interesting."

"Interesting?" She settled her arms across the mound of her tummy. "Don't leave anything out."

But I was going to leave something out. She didn't need to hear anything about my time with Ryan or about my talk with the Crimes Against Persons officer. It could wait until she was stronger and could handle the shock of Holly's murder. I was going to keep it as light as possible.

I pulled the visitor's chair up closer to the bed and told her about the call from Dan and about my visit to Dusty. "It will take old Dusty a while to walk upright. Then he'll be running out to get an HIV test."

"My guess is you've ended the friendship between Ryan and Dusty." She frowned. "Ryan is going to be very unhappy with you."

"Ryan is a weird one. No guessing what he'll do. I'm staying far away from him."

"If Dusty didn't know Holly was HIV-positive, and she didn't have the virus when Angel was born, is Ryan the one who infected Holly?" Her eyes widened. "Did Ryan knowingly infect Holly?"

She'd come to exactly the place I had. "Maybe."

"Do you think Ryan meant to infect Dusty through Holly or did he just not give a damn?"

"It's all too cruel to contemplate."

"All the same," Aunt Kay said, "if Ryan doesn't know Holly was ill, he should."

"I thought you'd given up interfering."

"Well, yes, but as you pointed out yourself, if we do nothing, bad things can happen as well. Then we're responsible for those."

"We can't win at this blame game, can we?"

"Not as long as we're still breathing."

"But volunteering can be good for the soul." I pulled out the check and handed it to Aunt Kay. "Wasn't it nice of Dusty to pay for Holly's funeral?"

Her monitor went crazy and I was asked to leave.

CHAPTER 49

I settled my sunglasses over my eyes and was hunting for my keys when my cell rang. Another call from Ryan? Or maybe it was the police saying that Ryan had been picked up and I could sleep without worries for one night at least. It was Cal Vachess.

Good news or bad, I had to know. "What?" I looked out the door of the hospital, searching for danger as I waited for his answer.

"My brother . . ." He didn't go on.

"What about Ryan?" My voice was stuck high in my throat.

"He's out of control. He doesn't know where the boundaries are anymore."

"No kidding!" I scanned the parking lot. There were no red Mustangs. "Are you just discovering that? And then there's his health to worry about."

He didn't answer.

"Holly was HIV-positive, and we both know she got it from Ryan."

"You can't prove a thing."

"I've been doing lots of reading online. Diseases have markers. Each strain is unique. If the police go looking they'll find out that Holly's strain matches Ryan's. He infected Holly. He should be in jail where he won't hurt any more women." I jogged to the truck.

"They'll never arrest him for that. It's too hard to prove intent.

The most they could charge him with is assault and in this case there's no victim to press charges. They won't even hold him."

I stopped dead halfway into the truck. "You've already gotten legal advice, haven't you? Probably have the lawyer on speed dial, primed and ready to go. You're as guilty as he is." I screamed, "Why didn't you stop him?"

"You really think I haven't tried?"

"So he just goes on ruining lives?"

"He'll stop."

"Yeah, when he overdoses or drives his car into a concrete barrier because he's high. And in the meantime he's out partying. How many more people are going to get sick?"

"Those idiots have to look out for themselves. They know the risks as well as you do. That's not my problem."

"Holly was never an escort, was she?"

He took his time answering. "She only went out once. That was months ago and it was a disaster. She ran out of the room and left the guy standing there."

I started the engine and cranked up the air. "And then what happened?"

He sighed. It took some time before he said, "She was Ryan's private property for a while and then he sold her to Dusty."

"But you said she called you."

"Ryan did. When Dusty threw her out she went to Ryan for help. He called and said she needed a job, said I should put her to work. He put the pictures he took of her up on the website but I never sent her out. I made her get tested, even took her to the clinic myself. That's how she found out she had the virus."

"She called you and told you that?"

"Nah, she told Ryan. He called and yelled at me for making her get checked."

"You wanted her to know. That's why you made her get tested."

"If she had it, she had to get treated, but I make sure all the girls get screened before they work."

"Ryan knew she had it and he was going to send her out there to infect other people. He wanted that to happen."

"That's ridiculous. I don't think he really thought it through."

"And I think you're just lying to yourself. Your brother is evil."

"He's angry that this happened to him . . . he blames people for things, and doesn't care who he takes it out on."

"He left me some sick messages. How much trouble is he going to give me?"

"His obsessions don't last. Just stay away from Ryan and give him a chance to forget about you. That's what I wanted to say. Go away for a while."

"How long do you think that might take?"

He laughed. "A day or two."

"That's what I thought."

"Take a holiday."

"You knew who I was when I came into your office. You saw my picture, probably heard everything Holly had to say about me. More than that, you knew Ryan killed Holly, gave her pills and watched her die.

"I bet he told you about it and you went over to clean up after him. Someone tidied up even before the cops got there. I think it was you. You're the careful one. You went through her things, maybe even took her journals and laptop. For sure you got rid of any evidence on her phone. And then you left that message on her cell, trying to get hold of her, in case the police connected Ryan to her. You wanted the cops to think she was just another sex worker. And all that bullshit that you were protecting me . . . you just didn't want Ryan to do another stupid thing and kill me because that would really screw things up for you. You're the brains, you're the one who does the organizing, probably delivering women all over the state. Well, your little empire is coming down. You better call that lawyer you have ready because I told the cops about you and you're going to be charged as an accessory to murder."

He hung up without answering. It was my day for having men hang up on me.

Ryan's messages were still on my phone. I could drive back up to Sarasota and take them to the police, but would they pick him up sooner if they heard what he'd said, heard his threats? And how long would Ryan be in jail after he was arrested? I knew the answer to that. Ryan would probably be out so quick he wouldn't even have to come down from his latest high, and unless Ryan was charged for murder, Cal would walk as well. What the cops knew and what they could prove in court were two very different things. I hadn't accomplished anything except to give Ryan a bigger reason to come after me.

Clay would be home soon. I held onto that thought like a lifeline. Things would be fine when he came home. I'd be safe. That's all I wanted now, to be safe.

CHAPTER 50

"You had your cell off." Brian opened the door even before I could get the key in the lock. He was beaming at me. "Clay's on his way home."

I sagged down on the chair in the foyer. "Thank god."

"I'm going out to the ranch for the weekend. I'm all ready to go," Brian grinned. "You and Clay are going to need a little space and I need to go to Lovey's Café for one of those heart-stopping breakfasts."

"Thanks, Brian."

"Do you want me to wait until Clay gets here?"

"No, I'm safe here. No one knows where I am."

He came over and hugged me to him. "Just remember, I get to be the best man."

I looked up at him. "How is it that you always know things before I do?"

"It's because I am the best man. Come on, I'll pour you a glass of wine."

A couple of hours later, after I'd told him all about my day, he threw me a kiss and went out to the garage. I heard the garage door go up.

My phone rang as I stepped from the shower. I wrapped a towel around me and headed for my cell, already getting angry at Clay for cancelling once again.

But it was Sammy Defino. He was calling to tell me he'd just heard on the ten o'clock news that Rob McCabe had been shot and killed in the alley behind his deli. Police were investigating but they had no one in custody and no suspects.

Even as I listened to Sammy, even before I started crying, I headed to the bedroom for Clay's revolver, hidden in the top drawer of the night table. I'd left it fully loaded, all six chambers. Both of those things were going against everything Clay had ever lectured me on about gun safety.

I finished talking to Sammy, swore I'd take care, and then I dropped the phone on the bed and opened the drawer. The gun wasn't there.

I stared in disbelief. Had Brian taken it? He'd warned me more than once about carrying concealed, told me that more people were shot by their own weapons than by armed intruders. But surely he wouldn't have taken the revolver.

I smelled his aftershave.

I turned slowly around.

Ryan smiled at me and said, "Looking for this?"

His eyes burned with a mad fire as he held up Clay's gun, wagging it back and forth in the air. The butt of a second gun showed above his belt.

I dove for my phone but Ryan was quicker, backhanding me across the jaw and driving me sideways into the wall. And then he hit me again. My head slammed into the drywall. Dazed, I crumbled to my knees.

His fingers caught my wet hair and pulled me sideways and onto my back. And then Ryan Vachess was on top of me, his fingers around my throat. His face was jammed up against mine as he hissed, "I saw the boyfriend leave with an overnight bag. Going away, was he?" He laughed. "We'll have all night. I'm going to take my time, going to really enjoy this." His hips worked up and down against me. He was already enjoying this.

He shoved the barrel of the gun under my chin, stopping my breath.

"You're going to pay for misbehaving." He got to his feet.

Standing over me, the gun pointing down at me, he kept me fixed to the floor with his foot on my chest.

I wrapped both hands around his ankle, trying to lift it and lessen the pressure.

He smiled cruelly and pressed harder, like he was squashing a bug.

"How . . . ?" I gasped.

"Oh, you'll see fast enough how I'm going to make you pay."

"No," I panted. "How . . . find me?"

"Why do you care? There isn't going to be another time for you to hide better."

I couldn't answer.

His lips twisted in delight. "A neat little device . . . a GPS tracker. There's no need to follow anyone anymore. Just put one of those on their vehicle and you have them on your computer. Of course the law says you're only supposed to put them on cars you own." This struck him as profoundly funny.

Still laughing, he took handcuffs from his back pocket and jangled them above me. My expression must have shown my terror because he threw back his head and howled in exaltation.

"You and Cal, so easy . . . and that fool who just left? Earlier, before you got here, he came back from next door and punched in a code for the garage. I was watching. No problem . . . just follow the pattern, straight across the top from left to right and down one. So simple, no numbers to remember, and he doesn't lock the door from the house to the garage. Did you know that? He just lowers the garage door. He likes life easy . . . so easy and so careless."

He reached down to touch my face and I bit him.

He jerked away from me, a reflexive reaction, and I kicked out with both feet, sending him backwards over the bed and onto the floor on the other side. I heard him strike the night table, heard his curse, but I was already on my feet, already gone.

Naked and running, a bullet sent splinters flying from the door frame as I burst into the hall. In the living room, a lamp exploded but I didn't stop.

Out through the lanai, bolting through the dark, I crossed the velvet grass without a plan. I just ran. Ahead of me, on the concrete walk by the sign, the long ribbon of moonlight streaking the water ended at a long dark shadow ten feet in front from me. The sinister outline rose and grew larger.

I stood very still, a monster in front of me and a monster behind me.

The silhouette in front edged towards me as I heard Ryan panting at my back.

I spun around and started pleading with Ryan.

"Please don't hurt me." Begging and being submissive was the only way to stay alive. And it was so easy to do. "Please, no pain." I stepped sideways, away from the water.

"Pain is only a little part of what I have in mind for you."

Inching sideways, towards the house, I edged away from the gator, while Ryan turned his back to it.

"Bitch. I knew you were trouble the minute I walked into Cal's office and saw you. But he wouldn't listen. Oh, no, he thought it was all in my head." He tapped at his head with the barrel of the gun. "But I knew I had to deal with you."

Slowly Ryan moved with me, circling around me, corralling me and herding me back towards the house. Now he stood between me and the shadow.

I raised my hands in supplication. "Please . . ." I moved towards him. "Please, I'll be good."

"Damn right you will." Behind him something moved in the moonlight. "Good . . . and obedient."

My hands went out in supplication. Close to him now, near enough to smell him, I jammed my fists into him, driving him down to my revenge.

He stumbled backwards, arms windmilling, but not quite losing his footing until there was a violent movement behind him. Ryan screamed. It was like no other sound I'd ever heard before.

Thrashing on the grass and then pleading for help, his hands stretching out for me, he was pulled backwards.

The gun lay on the ground between us. I didn't pick it up.

His fingers raked through the lawn as he was dragged towards the pond. At the water there was one more "Help me."

I watched the gator slip back into the water with Ryan struggling and screaming in its jaws.

There was a last shriek of terror and then the gator started to roll and Ryan disappeared.

The water was still roiling when the neighbors arrived, but only one snake-skinned loafer and the gun remained of Ryan.

A man said, "Why didn't you shoot it?"

"Leave her be!" a woman said. She wrapped some rough material around me. "You can't expect a woman to know how to do that." Someone else suggested I was afraid of hitting Ryan.

I gave a soft hiccup of a laugh and covered my mouth before the truth popped out.

The reality was I'd never be safe with Ryan alive. It came down to Ryan or me and I liked me better than him . . . simple self-preservation. Besides, Ryan and the gator deserved one another.

The wildlife people captured the alligator the next day. I never asked what was found in its stomach. I have enough nightmares with the things I already know. And I really don't think about Ryan too much anymore. I've got a bar to run.

The End

AUTHOR'S COMMENTS

For those who ask if this could really happen, here are the newspaper stories that set the little gray cells whirring. The first idea came from two newspaper articles in Canada about two different people who knowingly infected others with the HIV virus. The rest of the story was filled in by pieces from Florida.

On Tuesday, February 7, 2012, the *Herald Tribune* headline read, "After alligator kills, victim's family sues homeowners' group." Before this unfortunate event, ninety-one alligators had already been removed from the pond by the homeowners' association in the past. A representative said, "If you go walking around at night, you don't know what you might find."

Another idea: The same day, same paper, another headline read, "Pythons causing demise of species?" This article came from West Palm Beach. A growing population of pythons in the Everglades is causing unease and a fall in the number of raccoons, opossums and bobcats. Where constrictor snakes lurk, the population of these mammals has gone down as much as 99 per cent. My question is, when all those mammals are gone, what will the pythons dine on next?

I see another adventure in Sherri's future.